THE BURDEN IN MY HAND

BRYAN BECZE

THE BURDEN IN MY HAND

A MARINE'S STORY

based on true events

I have tried to recreate events, locales and conversations from my memories of them. In order to protect their privacy, in some instances I have changed the names of individuals and may have changed some identifying characteristics and details such as physical properties, occupations, and places of residence.

For information, contact *TBIMH2020@gmail.com.*

Front cover photo by Cpl. Tyler Main, U.S. Marine Corps, for the U.S. Department of Defense

FIRST EDITION

ISBN 978-1-7923-4248-6 (paperback)
ISBN 978-1-7923-4248-3 (ebook)

10 9 8 7 6 5 4 3 2 1

This book is dedicated to Kristin, who put me back together when no one else could. To our pit bulls Rexy (RIP), Athena, and Dakota, who showed me how to open my heart. To Rick and Maureen for keeping me from slipping into the underworld abyss in our youth. To my grandfather, Colonel James R. Kent (USA), whose extreme valor has inspired my warrior spirit. To all my brothers and sisters, past and present, in the United States Armed Forces. Finally, to all those who have served but never returned.

There are moments in our lives that we all cherish. I have more than a few that are book-worthy, but I've decided to keep those to myself, at least for now. So, why do I want to talk about the ones in this book?

It was important to me to share certain experiences with you, the reader, and let the people that were part of those moments share my trip down memory lane. Hopefully, if those involved are reading this now, they will remember with a smile, a gasp, or whatever comes to pass. After all, what is an experience if no one remembers it?

"Tumultuous" is the word I use to describe my youth, and more so once I returned from overseas. There were people in my life, past and present, which made a difference and made me the strong person I am today. This story serves both as a tribute to them and as a word of thanks from me. Also, it is a salute to those with whom I served in the United States Marine Corps, who were with me during times of laughter and great duress.

The events I describe are as I remember them. I have taken minor liberties and changed the names of people involved. Some of the people in this book are composites. This is a fictionalized memoir based on true events.

You will notice references to songs for some memories, annotated SOUNDTRACK: Band, "Song Name."

These particular songs were an influence to me at that time or just evoke the mood and memory of the particular moment. This is how I recall most events in my life. If you do not know the song listed, I implore you to look it up before reading further, to reap the full emotional benefit of my story. My hope is that you take away some of the sentiment from it as I once did, and still do. These are the occasions that have shaped me through the course of my life, and now I share them with you.

chapter one

RETURNING HOME

I was five when I knew what I wanted to be when I grew up. One night, before bed, after hearing my uncle speak of my grandfather's exploits in WWII, I became curious about the military. While scrolling through an encyclopedia looking for the section titled "Military," I accidentally stumbled upon "Marines." Alphabetically, "Marine" came first. My very first impression was a Marine wearing his dress blue uniform and the other various uniforms throughout the history of the Corps. From that moment, I was hooked.

I remember thinking that the uniform commanded respect and admiration. President Ronald Reagan once said, "Some people go their whole life wondering if they ever made a difference. Marines don't have that problem." So, at five, I was the only kid in kindergarten on future career day who actually knew what they wanted to be when they grew up: a United States Marine. For that matter, I am the only one who fulfilled their childhood dream.

If I have ever learned anything in my time on this planet, it is that life is a lesson that does not stop teaching. This was most prevalent with time. Time is a dangerously oscillating thing. When we don't have enough, we feel cheated. When we have too much, we worry, we feel bored and insignificant. It makes you hurt, it makes you heal, but most of all, it makes you think. It becomes a metaphysical revolving door that never stops turning. Two words have always summed it up best for me: *what if?*

These two powerful and haunting words can begin or end a person. They grab at your very being and tear apart your soul. Any shred of innocence that once was has now forever been taken from me because of this question. Every Marine who has been in combat asks himself this question constantly when he has lost a fellow Marine. This question has plagued me relentlessly over the years, but never more than in this moment. More so, we know that brotherhood can never be replicated in the "real world," because "loyalty" is just a word to civilians. So, you begin to ask yourself: *what if?*

What if I had been faster? What if I had been stronger? What if I had reacted differently? What if I had an ounce more endurance? What if I had been more on point? What if? What if? What if?

This is all I could think about on the bus ride from Camp Lejeune, North Carolina, to New Brunswick, New Jersey. It made the trip an eternity of "what if?"s. It felt like a constant knife in my chest, or an alien trying to burst out.

Perhaps, if the answer had been simple, Rick would still be here, but he's not; I am. It pains me, more than anything else ever has in this torturous world. I have often felt it should have been me coming home in a flag-draped box. After all, I was the tortured soul, I was the person who prayed daily to be released from this horrid existence. Nevertheless, here I remained, to experience yet another painful notch in my life. Rick was my guardian angel and I failed him. My name is Staff Sergeant Bryan "Beeznuts" Becze, and this is my story.

If you are wondering, the nickname "Beeznuts" was given to me in boot camp at Parris Island. Not because I have big nuts and am crazy, although I like to think I am, but because the drill instructors could never pronounce my last name correctly. Besides, I never feared death and figured I could only be killed once, so I was proactively creative with my sarcastic responses. This prompted the DIs to think I was nuts—hence, Beeznuts. To this day, people cannot pronounce it correctly. Every time I give my last name on the phone with someone, I have to use the NATO phonetic alphabet to spell it out.

To most people, flying would have been the easier choice, but it's hard to fly when you've been on so many military aircraft throughout the years. Anyone who has ever been on a CH-46E Sea Knight can tell you it's one of the scariest things you will do. I'd rather be back in combat than fly on one of those things again. From inside, you actually see the cabin body torque when it takes off.

Or maybe it was because I really regretted coming home. Though it's nice to take a break and see the country I so vehemently defended. The very same home I looked so forward to leaving eight years earlier. Eight years . . .

Eight years I spent away from everyone and everything that I knew growing up—aside from Rick. Now, returning only to bury that very same friend, my brother, my comrade-in-arms, I was not looking forward to this trip.

Camp Pendleton, California, was my home base, but we flew into the area around Camp Lejeune from

Iraq, with a pit stop in London, England, because it was closer to New Jersey. I flew with my platoon commander, Captain Kersey, and Rick's body in an ice-cooled casket via C-5 aircraft to MCAS Cherry Point. Later, at Camp Lejeune, the preparations for Rick's funeral began, and I was not allowed to stay with him. By order of Captain Kersey, I was to go home to New Brunswick until the funeral. He wanted my head clear.

Initially, I was going to fly, but I had an unfortunate incident with a parachuting jump not too long before that, in Iraq, which I'll tell you about later. So I chose ground transportation. At first, the bus trip seemed like a good idea, to clear my mind. However, it took an eternity, and all I had been doing was reflecting; a poison if it ever was.

Reflecting on time growing up, time with friends, time in Iraq—and, most troubling, the time spent on the "what if?"s. People have always told me that the past is the past and there is nothing you can do to change it. As people always say in New Jersey, "It is what it is." Therein lies the problem: no Marine ever forgets the past. We are bred from boot camp to remember it.

Three stops I had already completed on this smelly Greyhound bus with people that never seemed to shut the fuck up. I was not in the mood to be friendly, nor was I seeking knowledge of those who wanted to tell me their life stories. I continued to easily end the conversation attempts during the trip with a simple "fuck off." Most people had an incredulous look upon their faces when I told them off, but they soon realized that it was quiet time I sought and quiet time I was going to get.

I tried to empty my mind and get into the rhythmic breathing my tae kwon do sensei taught me when I was younger: in through the nose, hold for three seconds, out through the mouth, one second. A little bit of relaxation began to come over my body. Finally, I started to fade out. I had not slept well nor truly relaxed since Rick and I were shipped out to do work-ups for the Iraq invasion ten months earlier. Even then, I had never truly been one to be laid back, because I was always aware of my surroundings and my mind never turned off.

It seemed every time I fell asleep, the anxiety dreams began. These anxiety dreams were like sick dreams: repetitive and shit I hadn't thought about in years. Those dreams were about my life when it was simpler, a little happier, and not so serious. Of course, my version of happiness was vast in comparison to most people's.

Unfortunately for me, I started reminiscing.

chapter two

1995

SOUNDTRACK: Run-DMC, "Down with the King"

The memories of high school began to fill my head, mostly of my senior year. It had always been my favorite. I had so many good times that year, but it blew by so fast that before I knew it, Rick and I were on our way to USMC Recruit Depot, Parris Island, South Carolina.

The year was 1995. In retrospect, that year was amazing: the food, movies, stores, clothes, and, most importantly, the Route 1 Flea Market in New Brunswick. For me, this was the first time everything seemed to move smoothly in my life. There were no major drama or problems, except for Vinnie, but that, too, had a great finale that year. This may have been a normal time to anyone else in New Jersey, but not in New Brunswick. To say the least, my life had been anything but normal. Then again, what was normal?

I silently smirked and leaned my head against the bus window. Finally, I faded to black. As I dozed off, I remembered the day I told Rick and crew, back in 1988, that I was a Boston Red Sox fan instead of the New York Yankees. It would have been different had I named any other team. Hell hath no fury like North Jersey people told that you are a Red Sox fan. At the time, I might as well have told everyone I was coming out of the closet, which at the time was also taboo. I had to have been the only Red Sox fan in New Brunswick—or the state, for that matter—and damned if I did not pay for it dearly every season.

To be a Red Sox fan in a Yankee town is sacrilege. Sure, you had your Mets fans, and they did embarrass the Red Sox in '86, but they relented and gave respect. However, if assholes could fly, Yankee Stadium would be the airport. Every series between the Red Sox and Yankees was time to duct-tape me to a chair or the porch, or to execute any other fucked-up idea spawned by the rest of the neighborhood for their enjoyment— provided the Yankees won. Then again, the neighborhood would do it anyway, regardless of who won, just out of spite. Sometimes they would even throw beanbags at me while I was taped up, just to add to the fun. Fruit and tomatoes were also fair game for toss. The bodega owner looked forward to it, because he sold more produce on those days than any other time during the year, and the sales were constant throughout baseball season.

One time, I was duct-taped to an office chair and rolled down the street while everyone was cheering and throwing lettuce and tomatoes at me. The architects of this display had me bumping into random inanimate objects strategically staged along the way. Pain is weakness leaving the body.

Now, occasionally, Rick would "get a feeling," and it would inspire them to grab a few eggs to be artistic. Another time, they smeared peanut butter on my face as I was wheeled down the street with a flannel comforter duct-taped around me in the middle of July just to make it interesting. It was like clockwork, every series, and I could count on it.

I was always on guard when the series ended, so that I would not be sacrificed to the Yankee Baseball Gods. One could say it was like Cato from the *Pink Panther*, always attacking Inspector Clouseau unexpectedly when Clouseau entered his own apartment.

I was sort of the village idiot in that regard. However, I never gave an inch, because fuck you, I'm going down fighting. It is better to die on your feet than to live on your knees. The Red Sox Nation does not need a reason and we don't surrender. I will go down fighting for what I believe in, especially when it comes to baseball. As painful as it was, I always made them work for it, each and every time, with more ferocity than the time previous.

Eventually, my strategy paid off and they got worn out trying to tie me up. I took the fun out of it, I guess. After a while, being a Red Sox became accepted. I finally was the only person in my neighborhood allowed to walk down the street wearing Boston Red Sox apparel without issue or provocation. It was earned. Alas, I digress. Back to 1995.

These were good times, but my thoughts always shifted back to a more complex happiness: Maureen Calderra. Maureen was Rick's older sister by about a year and a half, and she kept us protected outside of the parents' eye: a guardian of sorts. She had been able to get her own apartment while she was attending Rutgers University, of which Rick and I took full advantage. It was our home away from home away from the rest of the world.

That was a sense of freedom I had not yet experienced. If I was having a rough day, I would always sneak in through her window and talk to her for an hour or two. She didn't mind one bit, because, unbeknownst to me, she had some serious feelings for me since I first met her when we were kids. Out of respect for my and Rick's friendship, she did not want to complicate things, so she never told me. That was, of course, until the week before Rick and I were shipping off to boot camp.

For me, she was always the beautifully intelligent woman that was physically fit from playing field hockey her whole life. I was completely oblivious to her signals and always thought her just to be really friendly because I was sort of family. Alas, the village idiot strikes again.

Women never revealed their attraction to me. I found out many years later that the friendliness I felt from women was something else, and quite a few women showed their disdain for my failure to pick up their hints. Who knew? I was a man. News flash, ladies, we men are simple creatures that need to be told directly or we won't figure it out. Be blunt.

That had to have been one of the greatest weeks for me, right before shipping off. I have never burdened myself with regret in this life, save one: Maureen. I have always cared for her, and, without realizing it, I had always used her as the standard for the girls I dated. All of my ex-girlfriends hated Maureen, because they could read her like a book and she did not hide her feelings. Not only that, she was overly protective of me for a reason that I was never able to fathom. Also, she was never fond of them, either, any of them, and that should have been a sure sign. Still, I never once picked up on it.

The fact was that I had never found anyone good enough or that made me happily nervous with butterflies, or whatever gives people that "goosey" feeling. At one point, I almost thought something was wrong with me. That same feeling you get when you are blown away and left speechless by the other person, like a sucker punch to the stomach or so the Hollywood movies tell us. I never experienced it.

My ex-girlfriends would tell you I was callous and apathetic. I normally considered my ex-girlfriends to be tools. No, more like hardware stores. One looking outside in would have probably called me a player, but this was a misunderstanding, and none of my ex-girl-friends ever understood it. They saw it as a rejection. This was somewhat true, but it took a lot to woo me: I don't settle.

I once confided these standards to Maureen, oblivious to her interest. She always told me to never settle and to keep looking until I found the "one." She would continuously ask me, jokingly, whenever I came over, if I was still searching, to which I always replied, "Always and forever."

Time was running out for Maureen, and she needed to tell me how she felt, because she had an eerie feeling that she would never see me again. She later told me she had fallen for me in 1987, when I moved in with her family. The moment she saw me brought into her family's house by Social Services, she was swept away. I had always felt like her little brother. The feeling never lessened, only strengthened over time.

To her credit, this woman had endured watching me date other women and overhearing me telling Rick about my exploits. It drove her nuts. She later told me it felt like pins were pricking her heart when I would talk about them, but it felt like a dagger stabbing her heart when she would see me with them out and about.

I, being a knucklehead, never picked up why there was a firm rule about me not bringing my girlfriends over to her place, but Rick could. Maureen called her place a sanctuary that need not be desecrated by the "hookers" I dated.

Now was the time, and time was short. Rick and I were set to leave for MCRD Parris Island, South Carolina, in a week. Maureen was beginning to panic. This was going to be her moment to finally get me to notice; she was determined to blow me away. She would succeed, come hell or high water. Mind you, this was all told to me after the fact. You can't make this shit up.

Her moment came when she heard that Rick and I were hanging out with a bunch of friends at the local pub down the block, called Shenanigans. Aptly named, it was the neighborhood bar that all the locals went to, to unwind after work. The head bouncer, Nick, would always give me a hard time about getting into the bar. I never understood his contempt for me. Maybe it was because I was pretty, but I don't know, nor did he ever reveal it. He once denied me entry "because it was a place for men to hang out, not kids." What a punk.

Nick was a former Marine who served in the Persian Gulf War, which many had thought made him the angry man he was all the time. Deep down, I knew he had a heart of gold, at least I liked to think he did. However, Nick would always make me wait while everyone else would go in, and would come up with some new and inventive way to screw with me. Okay, maybe he didn't have a heart.

At the bar, Rick and I were with our two other friends, Tim Walsh and Jim "Beano" McNish. Tim was a smaller guy who always got picked on by our neighborhood adversaries, Vinnie and his crew. Tim never complained about it, not once, not even to us. You see, there were no anti-bullying laws back then: men had to be men.

Vinnie normally respected Tim's ability to keep his mouth shut, but he still would occasionally do something stupid, like throw Tim in the trunk of his car and then drive down the worst-potholed street in New Brunswick. Why? Because Tim was small. However, this made Tim use his brain to make up for his lack of brawn. It was his smarts that usually kept us guys out of bad situations, as he was the brains of our outfit. He was the only one of our group to get into college, an Ivy League one at that. He had a full ride at Columbia University in the fall.

Jim was the practical joker of the group. Suitably appointed, he earned the nickname "Beano" because he had the worst case of gas anyone had ever heard—or smelled, for that matter. It was uncontrollable for a long time while we were growing up. Seriously, it was clinically diagnosed. I don't remember the exact condition he was diagnosed with, but it made for a good time. We pitied the people who sat next to him in class.

Study hall would sound like cats screaming and trumpets playing out of sync as it echoed throughout the cinder-block classrooms. These flatulent fits would last a good ten minutes at a time. He made it a point to harness this unappreciated gift by controlling his sphincter muscles and making songs, to hone his ability as if it were a superpower. Some kids would have been embarrassed by this, but it only encouraged harnessing his fractal aromatic rectal tremor (FART) powers all the more.

It wasn't until a doctor suggested Jim take Beano that his flatulence finally died down. Jim always figured making people laugh would take the spotlight off his issue, and it did. To this day, he makes his farts into an artistic impression—almost like a concerto, as it were. Beano always made people smile, no matter the situation. He would always be in character, which could get annoying as hell at times, but nonetheless, we loved the guy.

The four of us were talking and laughing at the corner table. The dance floor had opened up and people were dancing all around, having a good time. In hindsight, I have always associated some song, movie, or smell with a certain memory. It is how I am wired and I have a hell of a recall to this day.

SOUNDTRACK: Montel Jordan, "This Is How We Do It"

The crowd was getting down on the dance floor. You always "got down" when that Montel jam came over the speakers. One cannot resist the positive vibes this song gave off, and I don't give a shit how bad a mood you were in, this song would put you in a good one. Anyone would dance when it was played, even the seat-dancers. If you did not know, seat-dancers are the people that only dance in their seats.

Rick and I were at our regular place, and I was seat-dancing on my chair in the corner facing the dance floor. I always faced the front door of the place. Constantly aware of my surroundings, I was always looking around, just because you never know. I had been beaten up a few times in the past because I did not pay attention. Thomas Taylor said it best in 1617 AD: "Experience is the best teacher." Besides, as a guy with raging hormones, I wanted to know when a hot girl was walking into the place.

Rewind some years. As I stated, I had been beaten.

This awareness was now a forced instinct, because I was jumped by the same seven black kids every week in junior high. They called themselves "The Seven." It went on and on for months and I never knew when these mongrels would strike. That was, of course, until the day I figured out if I grabbed one of the little bastards and beat on him while the others were pounding on me, that guy would not return the next time. Thus I had put this theory into action.

It turned out my hypothesis was correct. Physical harm deters many, even the strongest. Every week I took a beating, but each one brought me closer to the final bout. Each time, one of those bastards went down with me like clockwork: six, then five, then four, and finally three. Happily, I was winning! Between the beatings from my drunken dad and the Seven, I built up Teflon skin and concrete fists. Therefore, my reputation in the neighborhood began to rise.

Finally, the last three were now wary and rightfully so, but this was going to be the final day of this shit. When it began, I took a few shots, as always, but soon after I became victorious. This serpent had lain in coil long enough, and I beat them down, hard.

Someone actually called the police afterwards, because of the damage I inflicted. Let that resonate for a moment. When the police came to question me after the fact, they informed me that all three of the last Seven had been taken to the hospital for broken bones and severe internal injuries. At that moment, I thought I was going to be arrested until the cop repeated what they said: "He just kept coming no matter how much we went at him . . ."

To their credit, they admitted to everything. I guess it was penance for their guilt, or rather the shame of one white boy getting the better of all three of them at the same time. To this day, I always have eyes in the back of my head. Somehow, I just knew one day it would save my life. Still, the sheer looks of terror on the remaining Seven when I retaliated were well worth the hits I had taken. I would have laughed when the cop told me, but I chose to be coy.

Never, from that moment on, have I ever lost a fight. Eventually, people stopped challenging me. I was the champion of the neighborhood, with the exception of Vinnie. We were like Holyfield and Tyson before both Tyson and Vinnie went to jail. The tension was there, but we never fought. A few times we came close, yet it never came to fruition. I guess we were both scared of losing our titles. Respect was a powerful thing back in those days. It was earned. Unlike these days, with the safe-space cradles.

Fast-forward back to the bar. I continued to survey the room and Rick nudged me to relax a little. There was no reason for my nervousness. After all, we were in our meeting house. Still, I kept an eye out. Then I saw her.

SOUNDTRACK: Everything But The Girl, "Missing (Todd Terry Remix)"

This girl walked into the place. It was like a supernatural force compelled me to watch as she entered, and I could not turn away. I could not see her face, but I knew for certain, from her silhouette, that she had an amazing figure. This perfectly shaped vixen slowly maneuvered across the dance floor towards us. Try as I did, I could not fully make out her face, but whoever she was, I could tell she was all that and chicken fat.

I was able to see that she was wearing a black skirt that came down right above her knees, and had an amazing set of legs. Her walk across the floor commanded acknowledgement of her sexuality. It was by this time that the other fellas homed in on her, too. Inquiring minds wanted to know, who was this woman?

When Maureen reached our table, she had us boys staring in disbelief; some of us even had our mouths open. Cordially, she asked to join us, and not a word was uttered as we all stared while she pulled up a chair. Rick was clearly displeased by her miniskirt, but she reminded him that she was the older sibling. Additionally, she reminded Rick that he was underage. Regardless, his anger was apparent. Leave it to Beano to say the first douche-bag line, "Did you have Lucky Charms for breakfast? Because you look magically delicious!"

Rick was quick to smack Beano upside the head. My mouth was half open and I was still in shock. I had never seen Maureen like this before. Her eyes seemed greener and brighter than ever, her lips fuller, and her legs . . . Hey, I was always a leg guy and she knew it.

Truly, I felt like the wind had been knocked out of me, especially when she looked over at me and wickedly grinned. A warm rush swelled through my body and it bothered me, because there was no controlling it. This was an unusual sensation to me, as I had never felt this out of control before. When she began to speak to me, I felt a strange sensation in my stomach, one I had never felt before. This was ridiculous.

I had known this girl since I was eight years old, or at least I thought I had, and even my speech became stammered a few times. A lack of concentration will do that. To say I was feeling beyond nervous was an understatement.

Thankfully, nobody seemed to notice, except for Maureen. She always noticed that shit, and she could not help but blush every time I looked at her. Still, being my goofy self, I had to relent a little. I had to give her a small grin, one that she knew. She had seen it before, but only directed at other women. However, Rick was wary and not pleased at all.

As it started to get more crowded, Rick suggested we all go to the Limelight over on Sixth Avenue at West 20th Street in Manhattan. It was a thirty-minute trip into New York City from the New Brunswick train station. I loathed the Limelight and immediately said no. Many times, I had been subjected to weirdness there and I did not want to surround myself with a bunch of circus freaks. Granted, the music was always good and the transvestite doorman always well dressed, but I had to be in a certain mood to go to that place. Limelight, like Studio 54, was where morals went to die. For Christ's sake, the club was in a former church. What more need I say?

Now, I am a Guido at heart. I loved, and still love, house music. I think it is ingrained in the DNA of people from North Jersey. After all, I had a huge crush on Anita Doth from the group 2 Unlimited. You know them as the folks that did songs like "Twilight Zone," "No Limit," "Tribal Dance," "Get Ready for This," and "The Real Thing." I am all about bass thumping, but you have to be in a mood for that shit, and this wasn't one of those times.

Maureen said she was waiting for a friend and they were going to go uptown later. I offered to wait with her until her friend arrived. Rick did not think anything of it because he knew I hated Limelight. Besides, he did not want to leave his sister by herself, certainly not looking the way she did. If he had only known what impure thoughts I was having at the time.

Beano, Tim, and Rick all got up and left after doing their ritual handshakes with me. That's how we did it. The victory bell had all but sounded, and finally Maureen had her moment. I still had no idea what was happening, but I was taking it as it came. She was cautious to allow enough time for the other three to leave and make sure they were not coming back. Then she looked at me with this look I can only describe as sultry, and leaned over coyly to tell me that her friend was not coming. Startled, I looked at her with a sly grin on my face.

"You dirty little minx," I joked.

At that point, I was a little tipsy, but I was more than willing to play along. What's the worst that could happen? She was my de facto sister, so it seemed somewhat odd that I was feeling the way I did. Maybe I was just an overly hormonal guy. Lord knows I had plenty of teachers tell me that over the years. Maureen suggested I take a walk with her, and happily I complied. So we grabbed our things and left.

Casually and slowly, we walked down the sidewalk, side by side, engrossed in conversation. I was never this conversational with anyone, even Rick. There was a solace I found in talking to her that I could not get from anyone else. She was always easy to talk to and one of the few people in whom I regularly confided. Other people thought I was reserved, quiet, somewhat dangerous, and enigmatic. I was dangerous, but only if pushed.

It was a warm night, and the stars were actually visible for once through the pollution of Middlesex County. In truth, it was the first time I appreciated the stars. We talked the whole way to Maureen's apartment building. When we arrived, words escaped us and it became quiet. It seemed there was a feeling of playful awkwardness that existed between us. I was having a great time and did not want to leave, nor did I want it to end. This was going great and I had never felt more comfortable in a long time.

Like an ADHD kid on Fun-Dip, I began to ramble about random topics. Maureen just kept standing there, smiling at me without saying a word, as if everything I said went in one ear and out the other. She gave me a look like I was talking too much. This feels like a date, I thought, but fuck it, I'll ask anyway, "Can I come up?"

Without hesitating, she said yes, as if she had been waiting for me to ask the whole night. Up we went. I was cautious to not give away the fact that I was, for the first time, checking out her buttocks as she walked up the stairs. It was magnificent: firm but abundant. I had never noticed its perfect contour before this moment. Odd.

It is funny, the things you don't notice when all the while they've been right there in front of you. It's a touch, a smell, or a taste that sends you spiraling away from your comfort zone, then places you into a new realm that was always there. I liken it to the tesseract. I was too obtuse to pick up on it. Check out Carl Sagan's explanation on the fourth dimension to understand my point.

Inside, while Maureen was grabbing something to drink for the both of us, I had a chance to curiously look over all the pictures on her mantle. Funny, I never noticed before how many pictures of me were up there, even more than her brother Rick's. Confused, I wondered why someone would keep all these pictures . . . Unless . . .

It began to dawn on me for the first time. Finally,

the village idiot started to see the signs. As I realized it, my heart started pounding. She had been at it all these years. Silently waiting for her turn, she had kept it together. Regardless, I had never been afflicted like this by a woman.

As she strolled in with my drink in hand, she said, "A lot of good memories."

I nodded. She turned dangerously close to me, staring directly into my eyes. I was intimidated. My heart began pounding and I tried to keep my composure. For all my hard-assness, I was failing in that department for the first time. I was supposed to be the tough one, the person that our crew looked to for strength. It was overwhelming.

I put the glass down on the mantle and moved away, frustrated. Maureen, surprised, asked if something was wrong, because I was now starting to pace around her living-room table.

"Yeah," I scoffed, but continued with some hesitation, "All night, all night with you."

"All night what?" She shrugged.

"This, this thing you're doing with the black skirt, the eyes, everything. You're stirring me about," I said. "What is this?"

Maureen's face dropped. She now looked panicked, walked over to me, grabbed my arm, and said, "What do you mean? I wasn't trying to mess with your head, or . . . or confuse you."

"Well, you failed. I haven't been able to think straight all night. My chest is fucking pounding whenever you come near me. My . . . my stomach is in knots when you look at me. I don't know what I am feeling, but this shit is not kosher. I-I-I feel so, what the fuck? Is this a panic attack?" I belted out.

Maureen put her hands on her forehead and gave out a sigh of relief. I could have sworn, she almost smiled. Confused, I sat there, expressionless. She then walked up to me and said, "You really are a fucking idiot. After all these years you really never figured it out?"

SOUNDTRACK: Sarah McLachlan, "Possession"

Bewildered, I stood there, and before I could ask her another question, she pulled me in and kissed me. At first, I was surprised, but then the feeling faded and was replaced by a tingling sensation. It coursed through my veins like a club drug. Without thinking, for once, I returned it, passionately. For the first time, I put my heart into it and the feeling was so natural that my world of stress started fading away. As a gentleman, I will not speak of the rest of the evening.

The next morning, Maureen awoke to me sitting on the side of her bed, staring out of her window, which faced the street. My back was to her, but I turned my head towards her when I realized she was awake. Beautifully, she smiled as she stretched, and I gently stroked her hair away from her face. I wished I had known about this sooner. What if?

"I know that look," she said. "You're in deep thought. You don't think you made a mistake, do you?" She asked it as though she was prepared to have her heart broken. It seemed she expected a coarse answer, because my reputation preceded me. This time, I aimed to disappoint.

I looked at her and bobbed my head up and down. "Yes, I did make a mistake." Her heart must have sunk, as I continued. "I made a huge mistake."

She started to tear up. I looked into her eyes, then said, "I made a huge mistake by not doing this sooner. I really didn't know. I mean, really? Right before I ship out? Why the hell didn't you say something? I mean, not for nothing, but you know I am an idiot with this shit."

"Life is funny that way." She smiled.

"No," I said sternly. "It's tragic and this is yet another example. I'm now leaving the only thing that I have ever found to be pure. Seriously, what the fuck, woman?"

Maureen gave a look of shock when I said it. Her feelings always showed on her face, but she was overjoyed to hear it even though I said it abrasively. Overjoyed furthermore that it was an unexpected response I had given. She sat up and grabbed the back of my head.

"I love you too," she said as she kissed me, hard, then put her forehead against mine. "I always have, even though you are the village idiot."

About an hour later, after we had properly woken up, we were enjoying the breakfast Maureen had cooked. The joy of bumping uglies had started to wear off, and the thoughts of the consequences began. It ate at me all morning. Rick needed to know sooner rather than later. I was fiercely loyal to Rick, and I had never broken my loyalty to him—or anyone, for that matter—until now. I felt ashamed.

Nonetheless, it would have to be dealt with, because nobody was good enough for Rick's sister, not even me. It was also an unwritten rule that friends do not date their friends' sisters. Jesus, I thought, this is not going to be good. Then I heard it just as I was about to take a bite of my breakfast.

The footsteps were coming up the outside staircase rather loudly, as if stomping. By the delay between steps hitting the stairs, I knew it was Rick. I exhaled as I put my head into my hands.

Here we go, I am in deep shit and I don't have my shovel. All I could do was sit there with my head in my hands and wait. However, the pounding on the door startled Maureen. She looked over at me and let out a deep breath, as if to say that she knew the shit was about to hit the fan.

Rick yelled out as he pounded on the door, "Yo, you mongoloid muthafucka, open up! I know you're in there. I can smell the knock-off Eternity you're wearing, ya jerkoff!" The door was pounded upon a few more times before he said, "If you don't open this fuckin' door, I am going to shove a hoagie up your ass!"

Annoyed, I got tired of hearing him bang on the door, so I responded, "Is it ham? Because prosciutto makes my ass burn."

"Open the fucking door!" he yelled, not amused.

Reluctantly, I got up from the table and opened the door. Rick stood in the doorway, leaning on his arm above his head. His facial expression was one of ire. He looked at Maureen and at me, and then grabbed me by the shirt. I let him drag me downstairs to the front of the apartment building, because I hadn't a clue as to how this was going to turn out.

"So, what the fuck, dude? My sister, your sister? This . . . this . . . this ain't fucking Arkansas!"

"It just happened, Rick. And it's knock-off Drakkar Noir, by the way—" I began before Rick cut me off.

He leaned into my face and started yelling, "You think this is funny? What the fuck do you think you are doin' with my sister? How could you be with my sister?

Your sister, for Christ's sake! And how the fuck can you not afford regular Drakkar Noir? They sell that shit at Woolworth's down the street!"

"Some guy sold it to me for five bucks out of his truck."

After all his antics and yelling, he stood there quiet for a moment, and finally said calmly, "I am very displeased with your behavior."

"Huh, why?" I said, a little taken aback.

"This may qualify as incest."

We both looked up to her window and Maureen was standing there, looking worried. I, with a shocked look, turned back to Rick and tried to grasp the situation. I was still puzzled. "You knew?"

"I always knew, dumbass. That girl has been stupid retarded for you since we were kids. It was only a matter of time, dickhead. But damn, Bryan, I thought you would have picked up on that shit sooner."

Rick explained that I was a tool for not knowing. He then explained what I had already confirmed, as to why she had hated all my ex-girlfriends. I let him talk, because I already felt awkward and I also hoped he would feel better about the situation the more he talked. Moreover, I enjoyed his lack of eloquence.

"You sure you don't mind?" I asked.

"Look, bro, you are the closest thing I have to a brother. Nah, you are my brother. Even with the incest thing and all"—he chuckled—"I'd never approve of anyone else." He leaned in close and said softly, so Maureen wouldn't hear, "Just, just don't break her heart. The girl is really, really retarded for you. I don't want her waiting on empty promises. This is your sister too, bro. You know what I mean?"

I said, "Seriously, that is so fucking disturbing the

way you say that. My sister? The girl is amazing, dude. She always has been."

Rick gave me a huge bear hug, lifting me off the ground. I yelped a little, because I could not breathe as he continued to shake me in the air. Rick continued his annoying behavior by giving me a wet kiss on the cheek. This was male virility at its best. Ironically, Rick would be the first person to call someone a "homo" if they did the slightest effete thing. After he put me back on the ground, he waved to Maureen with a grin on his face. A sense of relief came over me, but time was short.

Every day and night that followed, Maureen and I were inseparable. Sometimes Rick would continue his antics by chaperoning. What a punk. Yet, be that as it may, it still was a great time. However, the looming anxiety crept in more and more each day for Maureen. For me, a cultured sociopath, emotions were easy to shut off. Not too many people in this world have had to bear witness to my quandaries.

To such an extent, this made me as impenetrable as a diamond: mentally, physically, and metaphysically. This, too, bothered Maureen, but I really did feel for her and her concern. It scared me a little, because it was the first time I opened myself up to anyone intimately. I could not explain it, but I always let down my guard around her. Not to sound corny, but she was the warm porridge at the three bears' house for me.

Like all great pains in life, the day inevitably came for Rick and me to head off. Maureen was visibly distressed. I, as well, was not feeling great about leaving her, and more so, I deeply regretted that we hadn't spent more time together. No sense dwelling on it. Too late again, the story of my fucking life. What if?

Maureen sat on the bed, Indian-style, facing me as

she tried to fight back tears, not able to look me in the eye. Eventually, she looked up. We sat in silence, looking at each other as she kept pulling her hair behind her ears. I focused on her face because I wanted to burn her image into my mind for all time.

I needed to remember her elegance, and her purity. Things I would not recall until I was in the thick of the worst possible situations in life. It was then, and only then, that it would become apparent. She was pure; the only thing I ever considered untouched by this shithole city in New Jersey. She was a pilgrim in an unholy land; a diamond in the rough.

Maureen could not hold back any longer and began to cry. I pulled her to me, tightly, to assure her I felt the same, but I never said it. I never could. This was an unusual feeling and it was not fair, I thought, none of this was. In retrospect, life had always been harsh and constantly teaching me unforgiving lessons. Pulling the hair out of her face, I looked into her swollen eyes. The smile I gave her made her feel a little better.

Without any forethought, it just shot out of my mouth, "I love you."

Maureen was blown away and, without missing a beat, asked, "Promise?"

"Always and forever," I replied.

Uh, what the fuck did I just say? Rolling with it, I could not believe that just came out of my mouth. I think I was more shocked than she was, but the truth was that I did. Normally, I would have caught something like that, but not this time.

"I know you can't call, but please at least write to me. I mean it. It'll give me something to look forward to as the time passes until you get back," she said.

That stung me a little. I promised to write and got

up from the bed, knowing full well that I was not returning. The Marines was my ticket out of this place. New Brunswick had been in my rearview mirror since I signed up. Now I felt guilty.

Rick was in the living room, impatient, trying to get me to hurry. Our Marine recruiter, Sergeant McJadden, was waiting downstairs to take Rick and me to the airport. As I was about to leave Maureen's bedroom, she grabbed me and kissed me, hard, one last time.

"I love you," she said, sniffling.

As I got into the car, I was able to wave to Maureen one more time. The recruiter took off like a bat out of hell, because we were already late for the flight. I looked through the rear windshield at her standing in the street as we sped farther and farther away. Off we went, to begin our three-month adventure at Parris Island. That was the last time I saw Maureen's face for the duration of my stint in the Marines.

Rick and I did really well on the ASVAB and were selected for the special operations school. Luckily for us, it started right after boot camp. So we opted to go straight there, forgoing any leave upon completion of boot camp and the School of Infantry. Maureen never understood this decision, but when you graduate Parris Island, you are exceedingly motivated. There is no higher honor than becoming an 0321: Force RECON. I never knew that my decision would affect me down the road, especially when we became 0326s: parachute and combatant diver–qualified.

I would normally get screwed by senior enlisted and was always pulling duty during the major holidays. Because of this, I could never get back to New Brunswick. It was the payback for always being a smart-ass. At least I had the Thanksgiving before I left for boot camp.

I was seldom granted leave, either, thanks to some damn hotspot that was always popping up. President "Smooth Willie" Clinton thought we were the world's humanitarian force. We were constantly being sent around the globe on a moment's notice. However, when Rick and I had the chances, we would get to Mexico, Canada, and so on. We typically stayed near the West Coast, because it was convenient to Camp Pendleton. Rick also rarely got to go home. I wrote, though, as I had promised, at least once every two weeks, no matter the situation.

Maureen constantly pleaded with me to return, but she never understood that it wasn't up to me. I would have called, but oftentimes I found myself in some far-off shithole with no electricity and no phones. Those were luxuries that would come much later for the guys in 2005.

The letters continued like clockwork for the first three years. We started off lovingly and sweet, but I became opaque after my first two deployments overseas. I was cut off from the world back home, at times for a stretch of at least seven months. The letters became less frequent, and my accounts more obscure, which worried Maureen, because she felt something in me was off. Then, around late 1999, in the midst of Rick's and my second full overseas deployment on the 31st Marine Expeditionary Unit (MEU), the letters stopped completely. The 31st MEU had an unofficial slogan, "No Need to Thank Us, Because We Were Never Here."

Unfair as it was, Maureen never knew why. When she was able to talk to Rick, he'd explain that we had been to some troubling places, but he would never elaborate, either, on East Timor and various other shitholes around the globe. Later on, it would be Operation Iraqi Freedom that would end up taking the ultimate toll on me.

For those of you who don't know, East Timor was some destitute island in the Indonesian Islands. It was nowhere in the world that a person would even care about. Yet there we were. All Rick told Maureen was that we saw some pretty horrible things done to the local women and children, and that we had gotten there too late. He also mentioned that as stoic a person as I was, even I had shown a reaction to what we had seen.

Rick advised her to let me regroup, because even he had never seen me like this before. It was a very rough deployment, and Rick only came home to see his family. He wanted to make sure that he was still living in reality and doing the right thing. After a while, for me, New Brunswick started to become a fading memory.

Operation Iraqi Freedom would soon be on the horizon, and it was Iraqi Freedom that would claim Rick's life. After all the shit that we went through, an honorable action was what cost him his life, and I would again be too late to the action to stop it.

Civilians have no idea and never will know what it is all about, nor why we do it. So, I no longer try to explain it to them. We cut off our family and loved ones from communication not because we love them less, but because we don't want to expose them to the real horrors that the rest of us have seen and borne. The world is anything but a chocolate-covered cherry. We don't talk because we want to protect you.

That was it, though, no more letters. It broke me up, but it was better not to expose her to what I had become. She had been my solitude that kept me sane, and keeping her at a distance would hold that vision cemented in my head, as crazy as it may sound.

She had tried to stay occupied so that she could avoid losing her sanity from wondering why. Even though she was heartbroken, Maureen never stopped thinking about me. She was crushed to know that Rick and I decided to reenlist for four more years. All she could do was wait and eventually give up.

But she never did.

chapter three

THE HOME LIFE

In my life, the bad times always outweighed the good. I previously mentioned my great adversary, Vinnie. Let me expand on this antagonistic prick. Giuseppe "Vinnie" DiMazio would give me shit daily, and I despised him so much. Given the opportunity, I probably would have made that dirty greaseball a ghost without hesitation. He was something of a Vin Diesel look-alike in all facets: the deep voice, build, face, and mannerisms. Most of the time he wore white tank-tops and a gold chain. He was the epitome of a hairless Guido. Furthermore, he was the embodiment of everything I hated about New Brunswick and, more so, New Jersey.

Vinnie was always provoking me, whether it was in school or afterwards; he never let up. He had heard about my escapades with the Seven and he wanted a piece of the local bad-ass. Two roosters cannot be in the same henhouse at the same time. The problem for me was that Vinnie had a black belt in tae kwon do, and he, too, had put all of his opposition down.

Again, there were no anti-bullying laws back then, and it was always about survival of the fittest. The two kings had to battle eventually, but as I said before, we were both scared of losing our titles because we were not sure about the outcome. He would keep up appearances to screw up my day by taunting me just enough to make it seem to everyone else like he had the upper hand. But I got my vengeance eventually and showed Vinnie I had craft beyond the fists.

One day, I devised a plan with Rick. In theory, it was simple, but the execution was not. The plan was to lock two hooks to the rear axle of Vinnie's car and make him give chase so the car wouldn't move. How hard could that be?

We needed to fasten a chain about fifty feet long and wrap it around the lamppost cemented into the ground. It would take a tank to move that lamppost. We had to do it while Vinnie and his crew weren't looking, and somehow make them give chase. It took Rick and me about two minutes to come up with eggs as the catalyst. So be it, the trap was set. This was to be the end-all, and I was ready for the fallout with Vinnie. It was inevitable, and we were all-hands-on-deck.

Vinnie and his cronies were sitting in his prized 1993 Toyota Supra in front of the bodega down the street. You know the Supra, with the ridiculous rear airfoil? Rick and I crept behind the car and secured the chains without being seen or heard, because they were too busy blaring the Masta Ace Incorporated's bass-shaking "Born to Roll" in the car.

After we carefully and quietly hooked the chains, we realized it was go time. We ran around the back of the bodega and cut into the alley, stopping at the front of the wall with just enough space to peer around and see the car. Rick handed me a few eggs and counted to three.

Out we ran, like a perfectly orchestrated ballet, laughing and screaming obscenities at Vinnie while we launched our eggs. They soared through the air like the last-minute touchdown passes. With pinpoint accuracy, the eggs landed on the hood and windshield while Vinnie and his crew stared in disbelief.

Rick and I took off down the street, running while giving Vinnie the finger. Predictably, Vinnie spun his tires so hard that white smoke was everywhere. Vinnie's anger blinded him to the police cruiser parked with two officers in the car directly in his path, watching this all take place.

The Supra shot out at rocket speed and hit the forty-five-foot mark for the chains. A loud bang that sounded like the twisting of metal rebar echoed throughout the block, scaring the people around us. The axle had separated from its host.

The car began fishtailing all over the road, strewing sparks everywhere. Vinnie and his cronies were freaking out trying to keep it from exploding. Panicking, Vinnie tried to stop the front end from crashing into the police cruiser, not realizing the brake lines had been severed when the axle broke off. It was too late.

After the car smashed into the NBPD cruiser and all of us finally stopped laughing, the police had noticed some noxious fumes emanating from inside Vinnie's car. Fire extinguishers were deployed to smother the residual flames. However, it just so happened, ironically enough, that it was pot. Boom, just like that, Vinnie was busted. Not only did they find half a pound of pot, but there was at least a half kilo of cocaine, as well. Needless to say, Vinnie was not going to be around for a little while. Talk about a bad fucking day, Giuseppe.

It wasn't until we were in boot camp that Rick and

I heard Vinnie had been sentenced to five years in Rahway Prison. It's not a good place to be. Still, I never felt bad, because I knew he would be out in eighteen months for good behavior. It was payback for all those years messing with Tim. To this day, Vinnie has sought revenge on me. I never gave a shit, because I never planned to see home again. I wanted to scrub my memory of that place. So ended the Vinnie chapter—at least for a while.

Then there was the curious case of Lazlo Becze, my father, who had a rough time in Vietnam. He was an abusive drunk who chased away my mother when I was a boy. Somehow, he blamed and hated *me* for it. When Lazlo was not beating on my mother, he would turn his sights on me.

One time, Lazlo said I was being a smart-ass and he slapped me on the back of the head. That slap caused me to fly forward and hit the side of the counter, getting a black eye and a busted lip. Two for the price of one.

Looking back, I think he might have been schizophrenic. It was like there were two people inside: Lazlo and the Devil. Unfortunately, the Devil was always winning. Rare moments of sobriety showed me a person I never got to know fully: a caring and loving father. Those occasional thirty minutes were what made me believe there was something good, something pure still left inside the crumbling shell of what was once a strong and vivacious man now constantly tormented by his service in Vietnam.

Still, Lazlo was more than abusive to my mother, whom I adored. I will never understand it till the day I die. She was an angel, my guardian. But everyone has their breaking point, and she hit hers, literally.

The night she finally broke free and left, it was rain-ing heavily. Lazlo had been beating her to the point where her right eye had swollen shut. Despite the many attempts to subdue my father with a golf club, I could not stop him. He was too strong from his days working down in the Elizabeth and Bayonne dockyards, moving heavy loads. It was like an ant trying to fight a bull.

My mom finally grabbed a vase, fought her way out of the house by smashing it on his head, and got in the car. She sped off, even with her swollen eye. Compounded by the heavy rain, her vision was terribly impaired. So impaired, she did not see the lamppost coming up fast. Not only that, she was not wearing a seatbelt. Panic had made her forget to follow the one and only rule she gave me for riding in the car: always wear your seatbelt.

It's funny how the universe always seems to take advantage of those ironic moments. It capitalizes upon the one moment we let down our guard. It is then that life shows us exactly how tragic it really can be. It shows you nature is not kind, and that good rarely triumphs over evil. That tragedy was the most painful life lesson I have ever learned and why, to this day, I never let down my guard.

The car slammed into the pole at about fifty miles per hour. She was tossed through the windshield, cracking her skull open on the lamppost. It happened so fast she did not even have a moment to scream. It was only four blocks down the road from our house on George Street, and I watched the whole thing unfold.

Drenched by the rain, I was able to run up to the car and see her slumped, lifeless body. Her face was unrecognizable; it almost looked like a mannequin. Her hand was still twitching. There was a creek of blood-water running down the hood of the mangled car towards the gutter.

I did not react, because I did not understand what was happening, but even at that age, I knew she was gone. I just remember putting my hand to hers and grabbing it tightly as the warmth drained from her body, until finally a policeman pulled me away while the flashing lights drowned out the scene. I did not cry that night, nor have I ever for that matter, and I had never spoken of it until now. I have always regretted not trying to stop her from driving that night. What if?

It was 1987, and domestic violence was not yet recognized as a crime, so of course there were no legal consequences for Lazlo. However, child services, or DYFS, felt Lazlo was an unfit father, because of the bruises on my body and his constant drinking. They had initially wanted to put me in a foster home, which filled me with absolute dread.

Luckily for me, my friend Rick was a very persuasive boy, and he talked his father into taking me into their household. Maureen was thrilled with the idea, but Momma Calderra, being a staunch Catholic, was none too delighted, because I had been born out of wedlock.

My dad was Hungarian and my mom was Scottish. Often, people think I am Italian and I have had little success trying to convince them otherwise. That being said, my heritage is basically a WASP. Momma Calderra was an ultra-conservative Italian Catholic. As a homemaker, she detested my homelife and upbringing, like I ever had a choice in the matter. She always thought that the trouble Rick got into was because of me; meanwhile, they were normally his ideas. Poppa Calderra was also Italian and a self-made stockbroker, who had done very well for himself. He was in Vietnam, but never spoke about it. He opted to stay at the house that had been in his family since the early 1900s. You could say he was very sentimental. Quiet, soft-spoken, but could make you move out of the way with the raising of an eyebrow. He was always very kind to me and knew that I would protect Rick if he got into trouble. Regardless, at Rick's pleading, they took me in as their own, and the State of New Jersey made sure that Lazlo's wages, whatever he made, were garnished automatically to help the Calderras with child support. Amongst all the calamity, the situation had worked itself out.

To that point, I have always felt that Momma Calderra resented me and thought me to be a vagrant, a burden of sorts. I never got an expression of approval from her, no matter how much I tried to please her with good grades or even an occasional gift. Rather, the only feeling she ever manifested towards me was when she was told the news of Rick and me joining the Marines, and that was one of anger. Mrs. Calderra hated the idea of Rick serving, and demanded, "What have you done with my only son? How dare you talk him into this?"

It stung me then, and it stings me now. She always blamed me for her son's enlistment, even though he was the one that talked me into it. Still, I let her think that was the case. It didn't matter, 1995 was almost over and I was almost out of this place. God, I had hated it there.

A bump in the road caused my head to hit the window and wake me up. It brought me back to the reality of 2003. It seemed hours had passed, and I was almost at my destination. It was mid-afternoon, and the sun was shining brightly. It was unusually warm; shorts weather even. Not much longer now, I thought. A sudden feeling of anxious anticipation began to creep over me. Not since going off to boot camp had I felt such uncertainty, and it was not welcome.

I took in the sights from the bus window as it drove through the borough. I spotted some old places familiar to me. However, there were more new places than old, which made it almost hard to recognize. To my chagrin, much has changed in the eight years.

Almost there, any minute now. The revolutions from the bus engine began to wind down, and the force of the braking made me lean forward in my seat: sort of like the plane landing on the runway. Alas, I was finally here.

As I stepped off the bus and looked around, I checked out my surroundings, like a prisoner just released from jail. I proceeded to take in a deep breath through my nose. Suffice it to say, this place still smelled like shit. Some things never change.

I had with me only my USMC-issued sea bag and one garment bag for my dress uniform. My outfits were pretty simple these days, unlike in years past, when I was a label whore. I wore my ankle-high black workman boots, blue jeans, black T-shirt, and car-length leather jacket, just in case it would get a little cooler. One might have actually taken me for a longshoreman or gangster. I did look the mafia part.

I threw the sea bag over my shoulders like a backpack, and off I went. I walked down a once-familiar street that now seemed a stranger to me. This presented a problem, as I no longer had any reference points. It seemed they tore down the old neighborhood for some new Rutgers campus buildings and luxury condos.

Consequently, I had not felt this alone in a long time. Where to now? I did not think the travel plan through, and just now realized I needed a place to stay. Rick had always been the planner when it came to this stuff.

I was able to speak to the owner of the old bodega, who still remembered me. I could not tell whether he was happy or suspicious to see me. Regrettably, I had not told anyone I was coming back. I think everyone just expected it. Regardless, he told me where everyone I knew relocated. It was within walking distance; not far, a few blocks.

This was a foreign concept to me. People had always said they wanted to get out of this place, but then the chance would come and they stayed. The real reason was because people were afraid of change. New Jersey has a way of sucking you in and letting you think that there is nothing else out there, just like Manhattan. I know, because I always had to pay a road toll every time I left.

I made it a few blocks from Lazlo's house when I heard what sounded like a familiar voice. The voice sounded garbled, almost like someone was being tortured. I hastened my pace towards the noise, because I always ran towards chaos. When I rounded the corner, I saw my old friend Tim Walsh getting roughed up by Marco Stanaco, Vinnie's right-hand man.

Vinnie and his crew pretended that they had some sort of honor code and always fought fair. This was probably true if you were in prison, and we know that prison has very honorable people, if you get my drift. Marco, a rather large and muscular man, had two other meatheads assisting him in his beating of Tim. What a challenge it must be to beat up on a 150-pound man, especially while two guys held him. Every time Tim tried to get away, they would throw him back up against the parked car and give him another round.

"Where's the fuckin' money, Timmy? Huh? Waiting . . ." Marco yelled as he relentlessly pounded on Tim. "I don't know why you keep looking around, ain't nobody around here gonna help you. Didn't ya hear? Your fuckin' fairy godmother ain't working today. So, where's the money? You wouldn't have no fuckin' degree from Columbia if it weren't for that money!"

I looked around and saw nobody helping Timmy. Par for the course nowadays. People stared and acted as if it was the norm, minding their business. What was wrong with these people? Then it dawned on me: North Jersey people. Always everyone for themselves. No loyalty and no honor, especially among thieves. I put down my bags, because this was going to get rough. The fairy godmother was about to get to work.

Welcome home, Bryan. Welcome home.

chapter four

WELCOME BACK

I walked across the street to the commotion and whistled to capture their attention. It worked. They stopped and turned to look at me. Who would be brazen enough to challenge them? A moment passed by, for them to size up this stranger, this soon-to-be-dead man. I stood before them, unflinching, brow unfurled, and fists clenched. My freshly brushed black hair showed signs of perspiration from the anticipation. A bead of sweat trickled down my face.

"The fuck you supposed to be, fuck-stick?" demanded Marco.

I pointed to Tim and said, "I'm his fairy godmother, and I came to work today, you pudgy bitch."

SOUNDTRACK: The Prodigy, "Breathe"

Marco looked for a second and thought very hard. Who was this man? No one was that nuts. He studied my face hastily and it hit him. A second glance confirmed it, and he said, "Well, well, well. Welcome home, soldier boy. Come and get your check, bitch!"

"Nah, nah, nah. That's where you're wrong, chief. I've already thought of three different ways to kill you.

You pose no challenge." I pointed to the muscle guys and said, "I'll settle for the two meatheads."

Marco looked at the first meathead and nodded in my direction. Meathead One started to move towards me, but this guy was an easy target before he even began. He hastened his pace, raised and pulled back his right arm, ready to deliver a forceful blow. I just stood there, motionless, waiting.

I would love to tell you that this was an eloquent symphony of flying fists, like in the movies, but real life is not like that at all. Jason Bourne is utter bullshit. It's either a few punches and then wrestling ensues, or the opponent gets knocked out quickly. Or, if you are highly trained, you know how to manipulate your opponent and get them to submit after they are on the ground, by grappling. There had been a few times since I became an adult that I had scuffles that were anything beyond quick. The fastest I put someone down was about one and a half seconds.

All the street fighting I have done in the past had always made me the aggressor. In the Marines, they taught me forms of aikido and jiujutsu. With the discipline of the Corps and the martial arts, these skills were drilled into my reflexes. Honing them as such, I learned to use my opponents' force against them as a defense measure rather than an aggressive one—effective, too. Beyond that, it all taught me one very valuable lesson: never be the aggressor when outnumbered. In short, these meatheads were done before they started.

With a lack of grace, Meathead One's right fist came in a downward motion. He did so by planting his right foot down as he swung to carry the forward energy into his right first. That being his mistake, I spun around in a circular motion to my left, planting my right foot in front of his. This caused him to miss.

With my foot still planted, I took my left hand and pushed it down on his back to continue his forward motion. As I locked my foot in place, Meathead One went flying into the car door behind me, knocking himself temporarily unconscious. His head dented the fender, and I later heard it caused a mild concussion. My move was subsequently described as a matador avoiding the bull. New best time: one and a quarter seconds.

Tim was still being held up against the car by Meathead Two. However, upon the quick dissolution of his colleague, he threw Tim down in frustration. I am sure somewhere in Meathead Two's mind, he had this victory all but won with one punch. After all, neither One nor Two had ever had a challenge up until this moment. They were the hired thugs, used strictly as muscle, not brains. These guys were dumb and only calculated strength. They never assessed skill, which became their losing move.

Meathead Two ran at me at full speed. As he came within a foot, he, too, was reeling up to unleash the fists of fury. Just as his fist was about to make contact with my face, I dropped down to his left in an almost push-up position. This caused Meathead Two to trip and fall forward, headfirst, and hit the ground, smacking his temple against the pavement. To his credit, he attempted to regain his composure. He would have had it, too, had it not been for my right arm swinging around into the back of his skull. His face smashed back into the pavement, breaking his nose—rather painfully, I might add.

There they lay, two meatheads, moaning and groaning in agony worse than a little child whose candy I once stole. Marco stood in disbelief as he surveyed the area. Hesitantly, and against better judgment, he decided to take his turn. He had to: Vinnie was watching. Marco was owned by Vinnie, and could not come back with a sob story about how they could not collect a debt.

I let out a quick breath, acknowledging the coming battle. Marco would not be so easy though; he was careful and observant. His only objective was to put me down, nothing else would do. It was principle, at this point. Sooner or later, Marco's patience would run its course and he would have to strike. That was fine, I had nowhere to be. I had all day.

I was already growing tired of this whole debacle, but I had to wait for Marco to strike first. He did not disappoint. Again, like the two that went before, he predictably swung his fist. As his fist came flying, I caught it mid-flight with my right hand, stopped its forward progress, then shifted my weight forward so that he fell on his back and I was now standing over him. This evolution felt like an eternity, but in reality, it was more like two seconds.

The one mistake all three of these jackasses made was swing with the right arm. Then again, how would they know to do anything else? Marco picked himself back up and was now more determined to continue. However, he was frustrated. Frustration can lead to doubt, and doubt would lead you to missteps. Even better for me.

Marco swung with his right hand and I ducked down off to the left, again making him miss. As I came up, I caught his arm in my right armpit, incapacitating it. My left fist swung around and connected with his chin. This allowed me to crack his elbow and toss him onto his back.

It seemed like one of those fast-motion-capture cameras slowing down the speed so you can savor the moment, like in a Guy Ritchie film. Picture-perfect it was, just like out of the textbook. My hand-to-hand combat instructors would be proud of my flawless execution.

Tim winced as he watched Marco slam to the pavement. Marco lay there, trying to get his wind back, almost choking while clutching his elbow enveloped in pain. I came down on Marco's diaphragm with my knee, ensuring that he would not be getting up. Victory achieved, at least for the moment.

Meathead One had awoken from his brief coma and realized what had happened. He decided to make another attempt. Enough already, I thought. I prepared for another round, and this time I would put this guy down hospital-worthy. Meathead One lunged.

"Stop!" yelled a familiar voice behind me. This was a voice that I was not expecting to hear. Meathead One immediately stopped, like a trained dog, and awaited orders.

That voice, I knew it, but from where? As it became clear who was walking up behind me, I could feel the anger burning through my veins. My fists became clenched, ready to go.

Vinnie slowly walked out from behind me. His eyes were locked onto me the whole time until he was facing me. Vinnie did a once-over of the area and what was left of his men. By now they were starting to pick themselves up off the pavement.

"Three of my best," Vinnie said as he turned his attention back to me. "I have known of one person that can dish out that kind of beating. But that couldn't be you, could it?" Vinnie got closer to my face, staring harder into my eyes. "That bitch flew the coop years ago, like the bitch he was. He wouldn't dare show his face around here now, would he?" Vinnie finished as he peered into my eyes.

Tim was still trying to process everything that just happened. With all my might, I held back. Don't take the bait, I told myself, don't take the bait. However, this was not my nature, and backing down was not in my creed, either. I nodded, let a small grin break from my otherwise stoic expression. This was going to happen sooner or later. Let's have some fun, I thought; bury the anger.

"You know, the last time I saw a face like yours, I fed it a banana. And another thing, quit breathing on me. You're killing me," I said.

"Come again?" Vinnie responded with disbelief.

"Not for nothing, I've seen people like you before, but I had to pay an admission. I mean, shouldn't you have a license for being that ugly? Careful how you answer, the zookeeper may hear you." I smirked.

Vinnie's smile retracted and he became clearly annoyed. He took a second to gather his thoughts, because it had been a long time since he had been insulted directly to his face. Vinnie acknowledged that I was not the same person that had left, and considered me clever. However, nobody disrespected Vinnie nowadays, nobody.

He reached around his lower backside, grabbed the gun that was there, pointed it in my face, and said, "You've been gone a long time, hero. Things have changed. People changed. Maybe you haven't heard how things are run around here now."

A searing heat swept through my body. I was self-destructive at this point, and a part of me wanted to make Vinnie pull the trigger. So I pushed the envelope. I put my forehead onto the barrel of his pistol.

"Pull it," I said, looking at him.

"Wah?" he said, bewildered.

"I said, PULL IT!" I screamed.

He looked at me again and said, "You're damaged goods, Bryan. You don't get off that easy. You cost me eighteen months." And Vinnie slowly put the gun down.

I took two very deep breaths and said, "I didn't come here for this shit, Vinnie. I am here to bury Rick, nothing else. I'm leaving afterwards. I don't have time to be bothered with your bullshit."

"That be as it may, you owe me for eighteen months. However, I'm gonna give you time to mourn for your boy. It seems he was a slick hero and shit. I'll let you say your goodbyes because when it's over, you will come to me. Your debt has not been paid and you will answer for what you did," Vinnie finished.

"Vinnie, it was a joke . . ." I began to plead, and he cut me off angrily.

"I don't want to hear your shit! I wasted away in that place. They treated me like a fuckin' animal! An animal!" Vinnie came in real close to my face and quietly said, "I give a SHIT about your problems."

Had this been high school, Vinnie surely would have thrown me a beating without thinking. He hesitated because this was a new me, a more confident me, and a seriously deranged me. Vinnie was even more worried about how unpredictable I had become. He probably thought I was just calling his bluff, but truth be told, I was wishing he had pulled the trigger.

Vinnie looked around, gathered his roughed-up crew, and they hobbled to his car. He told Tim to make his payment, then sped off. I looked over at Tim, who was now sitting up against the car on the ground, wincing from his injuries. I asked if he needed to go to the hospital, but he declined.

"Jesus Christ, I can't leave you alone for . . ." I started to say before Tim cut me off.

"I know, I know. You sure know how to make an entrance," he chuckled as he slowly got up. He looked at me for a second, and then gave me a hug. "It's damn good to see ya, boy!"

After I made sure he was, in fact, okay, we got caught up a little. Tim offered me his extra bedroom at his apartment. He had a second room that he used for guests anyway. Ironically, nobody ever visited. I gratefully accepted. To my surprise, Tim walked okay for a guy who just had the shit kicked out of him. He even offered to carry one of my bags.

We arrived at Tim's place and, after dropping my bags, I went to the balcony. I looked out into the street. People were everywhere today and it was a beautiful day, at least for New Brunswick. I could not believe how much this place changed.

I asked about Beano. Tim told me that Beano would be stopping by shortly. He also mentioned that Beano might strike me as different from what he used to be. Puzzled, I asked what that meant, exactly. It turned out that Beano had experienced 9/11 firsthand.

You see, Beano had been in the World Trade Center North Tower the morning of September 11, 2001. He was working on the eighty-seventh floor, only six floors below the crash, in the first building to get hit. Beano had a cushy stock-trading job and was working there early that morning to get ahead of the opening bell. I'll circle back to that later.

I asked Tim what the deal was between him and Vinnie. It appeared that during the summer before his senior year at Columbia, he was arrested for possession with intent to distribute at Sound Factory in Manhattan. Ecstasy was his product of choice, and he was making a ton of money. So much money, in fact, that he was able to pay half the buying price of his apartment at the closing. He was even paying his tuition in full as the bills came in. Unfortunately, he sold to an undercover agent while tweaking on his own product, violating rule number one for drug dealers who want to last in this business: NEVER use your product.

Tim pleaded no contest to the charges, and was sentenced to probation for four years. The deal was that his record would be expunged at the end of the four years. If he were to get arrested—not convicted, just arrested—for dealing or possession again, the judge would have Tim do the rest of his time in Sing Sing. Tim had explained to the judge that he was paying his tuition at Columbia with the drug money, and somehow the judge developed a soft spot because of it. All Tim had to do was stay clean for four years, and it would come off his record as if it never happened.

The problem was, now there was zero money coming in. The federal government would consider his infraction a drug conviction, and would not grant Tim any financial aid until the probation period ended. Tim had a cushy job lined up, where he had interned during his junior year, but he needed to graduate in order to nail it down. If he got this job, the financial rewards would be almost the same as before his legal troubles. But again, he had to graduate, and with no money and no job, the only person he could think to borrow that kind of money from, without credit, was Vinnie.

The deal was simple: $75,000 payback for the $45,000 borrowed if paid in one full year. However, 20 percent was added onto the remaining balance every year he did not pay the balance in full. This was doable if he graduated. Since Tim had taken a full year hiatus from school to fix this debacle, he ended up graduating in June 2000. He got the job in trading with the financial investment company in Manhattan, where he had interned. It was across from the World Trade Center's two biggest towers.

He was living the life. Payments were starting to flood into Vinnie's pockets and life was good. At least it seemed that way. The money he was making was almost equal to what he had made as an ecstasy dealer. If life does not prepare you for anything, it will prepare you for hard lessons. The lesson Tim learned was never, ever put all your eggs in one basket.

He was about to get his lesson. He started to explain it to me.

chapter five

A TUESDAY MORNING

It's funny, the things you don't remember in life because they happen in a flash. The trivial things, like a beautiful woman that just walked past and smiled at you, the scent of the freshly planted flowers along the street, the barista giving you a bigger size coffee for free, or the guy who let you take the cab instead of jumping in front of you. However positive these things may be, it's the worst moments that always generate total recall.

In horrible times, you always recall the explicit details that you never knew or realized existed before. A thing like it was a brisk, but beautiful Tuesday morning. The sun was shining bright in the sky and everyone was shuffling to work. The birds were singing and the sidewalks even looked sanitary. The trains were all on time. Everyone seemed to be in relatively good mood, even holding the doors open for each other that day. Damn, even the air was clean. This was the setting for a wonderful day.

In the office, Tim was setting up his daily schedule. The phone rang, and it was Beano. They talked about premarket values prior to the bell opening, as they had every morning for the last year and three months. Things were following their usual course. Then Tim heard it.

What the hell was that noise? Tim wondered. It almost sounded like the screaming engine of a low-flying jet. It couldn't be, he thought, no way it would come this low. Then it happened.

A loud boom came through the phone and Beano shouted, then the phone went silent. The vibration shook Tim's office building, even knocked his coffee mug onto the ground. He ran to the window, just in time to see the flames and glass coming out of the World Trade Center Tower One: the North Tower. It was 8:46 a.m., September 11, 2001.

"Jesus Fucking Christ! No! No! No! No!" Tim screamed as he hit the window a few times.

Tim was not certain, but it appeared the plane had crashed very near to Beano's floor. Tim frantically tried to gather his wits. He ran back to his desk and tried calling Beano, over and over. He kept getting a busy signal. What to do, Tim thought, what the fuck can I do? He looked around his office and saw his assistant, Becky, in tears. Not now. Tim grabbed his coat and ushered her out of his office. How could he get to Beano?

The sirens were already echoing throughout the area. There was rubble all over the place. Trash and burning debris were falling from above. The smell of burning fuel permeated everything. Tim made it out of the building, and now was standing directly across the street from the North Tower. The NYPD had already blocked it off, because people were panicking and bodies falling from the higher floors.

There were screams heard from above, as some people jumped from the burning floors. Tim watched in horror as their bodies, some still on fire, bounced, hitting the street. The sound was distinctive, like the sound of a watermelon dropped off a roof hitting the pavement.

The smell of seared flesh began to spread throughout the area from the now-charred cadavers on the ground. FDNY and NYPD did the best they could to remove them quickly. The smell was putrid, nauseating. It was later reported on the news that one person even fell on a firefighter, killing them both instantly.

The firemen were now assisting people out of the mangled building's fire escapes while watching for the falling objects. NYPD was doing crowd and traffic control. Tim kept calling Beano's cell phone number, but all he was getting was a generic recording.

It was now 9:01 a.m., and people were gathering around Tim. He was frantic at this point. His neck cramped up a few times while he was looking up. Tim continued to call Beano's phone when he saw what appeared to be another plane flying towards the second tower.

Stunned, he and other bystanders screamed in disbelief as the second plane slammed into the South Tower. The shock was overwhelming, and Tim could not muster any words. He felt frozen in time. The only thing he could do was stare at the inescapability of the situation. He put his hands over his mouth to silence his scream. The police and fire department began removing people from the area. Tim was forced out of there and headed back to his office. From there, he could watch to see if Beano came out. Slowly, he walked back, in utter shock.

In his office, Tim sat for what felt like an eternity, with his face glued to the office window. He hoped Beano would have the sense to head to his office, if— no, when—he got out of the tower. Word had already come down that the Pentagon had been hit by yet another plane. What the fuck was happening?

It was now 9:57 a.m., and it just came over the news channel that another flight had been hijacked, Flight 93, over Pennsylvania. He felt a sense of depredation that hit him right in his soul. He felt as though the USA had been raped, violated at a level never felt before. Tim sat there with his head in his hands. A few more minutes had passed and then came the rumbling.

Tim looked at the clock; the time was now 9:59 a.m. His entire office building rumbled as the South Tower began to collapse. The sound of iron creaking and glass breaking echoed as it crashed. Some of the bodies lay sprawled in the street, looking tossed like rag dolls.

Normally, this would have fazed Tim, but his mind was elsewhere. He could see some of the building collapsing from his window, but the dust and smoke soon enclosed the area like a fast-moving dust storm. As mesmerizing as it was, Tim still watched the North Tower. Through the cloud of dust and smoke that smothered everything like a blanket now, he could barely make out its outline. Still standing, he thought, Beano still has a shot, good.

It was now 10:27 a.m., and the North Tower started to sway. Oh no, Tim thought, oh no. Not more than thirty seconds later, the North Tower began to crumble. Again, the ground commenced to shake and the noise was unbearable. An off-white smoke layered the area and kept getting thicker. The people on the street were trying to get indoors for cover. Police and firemen had issued an evacuation order, but there still were a few that stayed behind, like Tim. Even the emergency services were ducking and running.

He sat down in his chair, drained. It would now seem that his friend did not make it out in time; again, inevitability. Eighty-seven floors may as well have been as far as the moon; Beano had no chance. Tim just sat there, looking out the window at the now white-covered street. Had it not been September, one might have mistaken it for a nasty blizzard. Tim began to accept that Beano was gone, and started to grasp the magnitude of what just happened.

Just as Tim was giving up, Becky came into his office and said a man was asking for him by name in their lobby. Tim leapt from his chair and ran down the stairs. When he reached the lobby, there stood Beano, getting dusted off by security. He was covered from head to toe in white soot, with but a few scrapes. Relief set in, he made it, the son of a bitch made it. Tim walked over and hugged him like a brother he had not seen in years.

"I thought you went down, buddy. I thought I'd lost ya," Tim said. "I'm sorry, Beano, I really tried."

"I'd rather not talk about this right now. I blame God and his lack of personal hygiene with the dandruff. I have to say it really is a good thing I am not a recovering coke addict. This white shit would make me relapse," Beano replied, yelling because his hearing was temporarily impaired from the building collapse. Then he chuckled while staring at the wall, dazed.

They both stayed in Tim's office the rest of the day and night. They were stuck anyway, unable to get out of the city, as were a few other Tim's coworkers. They made the best of it that evening, like a sleepover, but no one really slept. Mayor Giuliani had ordered an evacuation of downtown, but as it was, they were stuck. Amongst the massive numbers of NYPD, FDNY, official vehicles, and personnel running around, it was chaos.

When they left the building the next day, they both looked at what was now being called "Ground Zero."

They stood there, looking at the pile of rubble that now lay where the great buildings once stood. Neither one said a word as they turned uptown to the ferry to get back across the river to Jersey City. It took them about ten hours to make it back. Until today, Tim said, he had never spoken of the events.

The U.S. financial community was damn near destroyed. Two weeks after the event, Tim's company folded due to being one of the smaller firms. It took no longer than one day of the market trading being halted to send the investors running. By the Thursday's end, his company was bankrupt.

Beano had a little more luck, because his company had branches all over Newark, New Jersey, and New York City. He also did more work with foreign markets. Beano was stuck at the Newark office for the ten months that followed until they made room for him at the uptown NYC location. Regardless, the bountiful income that was once Tim's was now gone. When you make that much money, the unemployment compensation is equal to one dinner in a midtown restaurant.

Six months had gone by without so much as a call-back for a job interview. Now Tim began to panic. His payments to Vinnie became smaller and smaller. Tim had emptied every investment account that he had just to stay on top of his debt. He told me that he should have paid if off when he had the chance. Freelance work was not paying like it used to. He still owed Vinnie a balance of $30,000. If it was not paid off by January 1, it would jump to $36,000. And that was how it came to pass that Tim got beat up at least once a month.

I was stunned by what I had just heard, minus the debt talk. That didn't surprise me.

After Tim explained the events that led up to the

problem with Vinnie, Beano entered. It was good to see him, and he gave me a big hug. In Beano's true form, he licked his finger and put it in my ear as his customary greeting. Oh, how things have truly changed, I thought, laughing. It was good to laugh for once.

Beano mentioned that he overheard Tim talking, and began to add his side of the story. I guess my presence was enough for him to finally open up about it. He had been in his office, talking to Tim on the phone, when it started. From Beano's corner office, he watched the plane come closer and closer until it finally flew into the floors above him on one corner, and saw the rest of the plane come out of the other corner. He said the impact was so enormous that the ceiling tiles popped out and his windows shattered.

The heat that came from the ceiling was extremely intense. Down the emergency stairs he went. Beano hurried, because he could see the damage when he looked up and it was not a reassuring picture. Taking a leadership role, Beano kept the people moving despite their panicking and crying. He had no time for that shit, nor did they. He rallied them like troops and kept their minds focused on the door on the first floor.

Beano was able to make it out of the building without trouble. However, just as he was reaching the front of Tim's block, the North Tower collapsed. Nine seconds. That was all that had separated Beano from eternal sleep. Other than some minor cuts and bruises from the debris when the building collapsed, he came out unharmed.

Beano would never say how petrified he was, or how it bothered him. He would just shrug it off. But you could tell, when you asked, that he had been profoundly affected by it. His former roommate said told Tim that Beano had nightmares all the time.

"Jesus," was the only thing I could think to say because I was normally the one talking about fucked-up experiences. It was odd to hear it from the other side for once. I did not know what else to say to something like that. It did not matter though; it was relaxing time with the fellas.

No one spoke of the World Trade Center or exploits in Iraq. This was silently off limits tonight. The four F's were in effect: fun, friends, food, and fermented beverages. We had a great night shooting the breeze. I even indulged in a little inebriation. Beano did mention something about Maureen, but I did not rise to the bait. I was avoiding the subject for now.

"Are you gonna see your pops?" Beano asked cautiously, and Tim grew quiet, as if they expected me to get angry.

I just looked at Beano blankly. I did not answer, because I truly did not know. Besides, I did not want to scratch the surface of all that anger and resentment in this moment. That anger was best dealt with on another day.

That anger was perpetual and stored somewhere deep inside me. It was a metaphorical storage box, as my therapist always told me, and there was a weak lock keeping it closed. This box was there as a means of coping. It allowed me to not go insane from all I had endured in my life. Any average person probably would have gone crazy by this point. Lately, stress was the acid eating away at the lock, and it was only a matter of time before the box broke open. Pity the person in my vicinity when it did.

I got up and told the guys I was really tired and going to crash. We said our goodbyes, and they told me how happy they were to have me there, even under the circumstances. It was good to see them again too. But I had had a long three days and it was the first time I had the chance to sleep in a bed.

I had promised myself that if I ever survived Iraq, I was going to buy a new truck when I got back. After that bus trip, I wanted one more than ever. Most of my life, I never needed a vehicle, but using public transportation and bumming rides was becoming annoying.

As I was about to leave the crew, Beano looked at me again, as if he had been waiting to ask me all night, "Bryan, where have you been all these years, man?"

I thought about his question as I lay in Tim's spare bed. My eyes closed and I started to drift off into my anxious dreams. So quiet here. It was damn hard to relax when only weeks ago, I was in one of the fiercest firefights in Iraq. Beano's question kept echoing in my head over and over again.

Where have I been? Let me tell you.

chapter six

BOOT CAMP

I have always been very vague or apprehensive when telling people what I did in the Marines. It's a hard thing to describe; an experience like no other. One cannot explain it to a person who has never gone through it, it's not a good subject for regular conversation.

None of these experiences are what you would have in the "real" world as a civilian, and that is why the Marine brotherhood bond is so stalwart. Telling people who ask about it is like an astrophysicist talking to me as a peer about quantum entanglement. You may understand it, but you don't get it, if that makes any sense. I may be rambling here. Anyway, I digress.

I avoid the subject like the plague to this day, for the trepidation of people asking me how many people I have killed, or what it was like in battle. I always want to inflict pain on those clueless little shits, because it infuriates me to no end.

Real life is not a video game. Watching your friends die or get dismembered in battle for a politician's idea of peace or diplomacy through warfare is difficult, to say the least. But the worst of it all is having to be the one to hand a folded flag to the family of a fallen friend.

These are the same assholes who keep playing "Call

of Duty" or tell me they are "tough mudders." Snapper-heads. Real life does not give you an extra life after you have been killed, nor does it replace IED amputations and battle-fatigued, downtrodden spirits. Besides, we don't want to relive those moments with some little-shit hipster that hasn't a clue how the world really operates. And yes, we also pay taxes, so you can stop saying you pay our salary.

I'm always asked, "What did you guys do?" If you ask any active-duty or former Marine in the civilian world to answer that question for their corporate colleagues, they will most likely give the same answer: a lot of shit. Shit is our forte. We're given shit all the time, we live in a world of shit, we have to fight through the shit, the food is for shit, and the pay is shit. Yet we are undoubtedly "the shit." For Marines are not a unit in one particular area, even though our military occupational specialty (MOS) states otherwise, but we are the most multifaceted bunch out there. There is a reason they call us "the few, the proud."

So, why did we join? If not for showing our virility by proving to the world we were the ultimate bad-asses, it was for the uniform. Yeah, I definitely did it for the uniform. I'm told by many women that nothing is sexier to the female hormones than a man in that dapper dress blue uniform. It's the truth, and I am not being cocky about it. I have seen many women drop their britches to the ugliest of men wearing it. Those women were more than likely to have been inebriated at the time, but it has happened.

When I say Rick and I were inseparable, I mean it. The universe had dealt our cards that way. We went everywhere together in the Marines. We both attended the Third Battalion at MCRD Parris Island, School of

Infantry at Camp Geiger, Basic Reconnaissance Course at Coronado, and also various SOCOM schools. How does someone talk to Joe Schmo about being in Force Recon? People ask me, because Rick was always with me up until his death in Iraq. So, I have to assume it's either out of general concern or some sort of morbid curiosity.

I have always looked back on my time in the Marines with humor, because of the stress of it. If you let it, it will beat you down and take your soul. Rick and I began our Marine Corps experience Monday, November 27, 1995. It was a day that will always proudly live in my heart. Any Marine will always refer to it as "the day I stood on the yellow footprints." These are the beginnings of the transformation, but I'll circle back to that in a bit.

We started out at the Military Entrance Processing Station (MEPS) in Philadelphia. This was the facility where the Department of Defense screens people. They check medical and psychological issues, and also do extensive background checks. That is, unless you're entering the USMC, and in that case, everything will have a waiver. I will not get into it further, because the whole process takes about nine hours and most of it is absolutely ridiculous. They told us everything we were doing had a purpose, but I thought it was so they could laugh at us the entire time.

At the end of the day, we took our official Oath of Enlistment:

"I, (state your name), do solemnly swear that I will support and defend the Constitution of the United States against all enemies, foreign and domestic; that I will bear true faith and allegiance to the same; and that I will obey the orders of the President of the United

States and the orders of the officers appointed over me, according to regulations and the Uniform Code of Military Justice. So help me God."

Afterwards, we were all sent to our hotel rooms at the very prestigious Holiday Inn by the MEPS station. Supposedly, the aim was to get some sleep before we were sent to MCRD Parris Island early next morning. If you haven't figured it out yet, MCRD stands for Marine Corps Recruit Depot.

It was a restless night for the both of us. Fear of the unknown made us both edgy. At about five a.m., we were shuttled to the airport and sat around for a couple of hours before our flight to Atlanta. Why we were sent to Atlanta for a connecting flight is beyond me. I can only surmise that the government was again championing the lowest bidder. In this case, it was Delta. You always know when you fly Delta. Enough said.

In Atlanta, our connecting flight was spectacular, to say the least. We boarded this jalopy of a plane that had two propeller engines. I am pretty sure there was duct tape on the props, but we were hustled onto the plane as if the Delta staff were trying to cover up that little detail. The cabin was so loud that I had to request earplugs. I thought this made it worse, because my whole body was vibrating internally. Even the stewardess was wearing ear muffs! Christ, I even had to pay for my own soda, which was fizzing all over the place from the cavitation. Alas, it was a long one-hour flight from Atlanta. Again, Delta.

The sun began setting when we finally touched down at our destination. It was a decrepit, small airport in the middle of nothing with pine trees. Beaufort, South Carolina, was the name of the place. I was not made aware of that information until after boot camp graduation. But we were subjected to the Marines screaming at us as soon as we got off the walkway at the gate.

These were our liaison Marines to MCRD Parris Island. We were cattle, and they did not hesitate to yell at us at any given moment. Their job was to corral us as we came off the plane. They made us sit at attention on the airport chairs until told otherwise: left hand left knee, right hand right knee. Furthermore, they were kind enough to give us a "bag nasty." The final move was to put us on a bus bound for "the island," and by that time, it was already past midnight.

The "bag nasty," as it is lovingly remembered, is this brown-bagged lunch that consisted of, well, edible shit. It contained a bag of chips, a fruit juice drink with zero fruit juice (written on the container), and what I thought was an attempt at a sandwich. Oh, that wonderful ham and cheese happiness.

All who have tasted this piece of heaven never forget it. The ham was referred to as "horse cock." It was a slice of the worst government ham in the world, topped by something that once mimicked American cheese. It melted in your mouth and stuck to the roof of it. Ugh.

All this wholesomeness was assembled between two pieces of a mushed substance that once resembled bread. The two choices for condiments included in this delectable feast were either mustard or "salad dressing." This "salad dressing" was Miracle Whip in a packet. Which brings me to an important question, who the hell puts Miracle Whip on their salad??? When the "bag nasty" came around, it would be the only time you'd see Marines run from food.

We both boarded the bus, and our PI (Parris Island)

liaisons told us to get some sleep, because we would need it. Of course, Rick and I did not listen, a decision that would cost us our sanity later. We opted instead to chat and make jokes about our current experiences, as we always did back home.

The bus ride already felt like an hour or two, although I couldn't say for sure, because the bastards at the airport took our watches. But the giggling stopped once the engine of the bus started downshifting. There it was, the infamous gate: "U.S. Marine Corps Recruit Depot, Eastern Recruiting Region, Parris Island, South Carolina." It should have said, "Abandon all hope ye who enter here." It began to sink in: this shit was for real.

My heart was now pounding. The life I knew, of gallivanting and non-moralistic pleasures, was officially at an end. Well, at least for the next three months. You don't think about it when you are at MEPS. But it hits you when you pass through those gates and you read the sign that says, "Where Marines Are Made." Even so, the bus ride did not end there, not yet.

The bus went through the gates and drove for what felt like hours. Rick and I sat in silence, taking in our new surroundings, which we could not see due to the pitch-black night. My knuckles were white from gripping the seat handles, because I was tense. It may have been around two a.m. at this point, but I wasn't sure. They did this to disorient you in the event you wanted to escape.

The guy sitting in front of us was snoring away. How could anyone sleep at a time like this? Somebody wake up Hicks, I thought. Upon our arrival to the recruit-receiving building, a drill instructor was waiting to give us a true recruit welcome. The bus driver opened the doors, and on came this stocky, black drill instructor. He was a mean little bastard and very vociferous. The Smokey hat he wore was intimidating, to say the least. Allow me to explain why.

I want to be very clear about one thing: they are drill instructors (DI), not drill sergeants. Drill sergeants are from the Army and get called "drill sergeant." Drill instructors are God in the eyes of recruits and get called "sir."

We Marines are religious about this, because we fear and revere them. They are the meanest things on the planet, with Marine Corps running through their veins. No matter how tough you think you are, they make you shrivel. They are our fathers during the recruit-to-Marine evolution, and we take great offense when they get called otherwise. Try as we may to ignore it, we can't. It is like nails on a chalkboard every time some person asks me about our "drill sergeants." No disrespect to our Army brothers.

As we got off the bus, four other DIs began screaming at us to get on the yellow footprints faster than humanly possible. We all ran off the bus to line up on them. Of course, no matter how fast you are, you are not fast enough. I almost ruptured one of my eardrums when one of them screamed in my ear. It was a female DI, and she was loud, that bitch.

Rick and I actually chuckled when she got in my face. Her intention was to make us cower. Try as she did, it would not work. It seemed she had never met a woman from New Brunswick. She was mild by comparison, although she was kind of cute. But the six-foot-three, two-hundred-and-fifty-pound DI from backwoods Georgia, who hated city slickers, was a little bit more compelling. He needed only to grunt and we were more than happy to receive instructions.

Rick and I had heard stories at the recruiting office. Our recruiter boasted about them, as did all the fresh PI graduates that stopped by the station on leave. We were so looking forward to the famous yellow footprints. As sick as it sounded, we longed for this moment.

Finally, here we were. And there we went. There we stood on these historical footprints for a total of fifteen seconds before the DIs moved us into the receiving building. I have to admit, is was a little bit of a letdown. It was as if I was expecting some wizard to come out of the woodwork and have me pull a sword from the stone. Nothing to this point was as described by our recruiter. I learned one very important lesson that moment: our recruiter, Sergeant McJadden, was full of shit. This was not the time for this realization.

At receiving, we got shuffled into row after row of desks that were from the 1920s. I am sure the current Marine Corps budget only allowed for the recent buy of those relics as an upgrade. One DI gave a quick brief and sort of a "welcome aboard" presentation. The rest of the time, they made us keep our heads down on the desk, be quiet, and not move. The thing Rick and I both remembered the most was the smell.

Every building there smelled like it. I'd say the smell was the same as a brand-new semi-auto pistol out of the box. I can't describe it any other way. All I know was it was the strongest at supply warehouses and the armories. I simply thought of it as the military smell. After all the joyous information and paperwork had been completed, they instructed us to rise and form lines. Every movement had to be faster than the next. We were now headed to our haircuts.

Let me tell you about this bullshit. I am not even a

recruit more than two hours, and I am standing there waiting to get my hair cut off. The DIs line you up so that you can have the wonderful experience of having the skin separated from your skull. The barbers, if you can call them that, use dull clippers and dig into your scalp while trying to cut off any remaining hair. Not only that, they are complete assholes, who were also screaming at us. After the skin removal session, I was handed a paper towel and I leaned over a garbage can. In USMC terminology, it's called a "shitcan." Another recruit wiped off any residual skin, I mean, hair that was still there. I am pretty sure I saw plenty of blood spots.

We were shuttled into the warehouse and given— sorry, *thrown* our uniforms. There were Marines at each station, who launched our uniforms at us. It was like a quarterback throwing the ball as hard as he could from five feet away. These items included our camouflage utilities (cammies), both jungle and leather boots (Cadillacs), sneakers (go-fasters), and various other items. We shoved these into an oversized duffel bag. Cammies consisted of a blouse (top) and trousers (pants). The DIs then made us strip down and change out of our clothes into our fresh cammies and go-fasters. Boots were not yet necessary. At this point, the sun was starting to rise and we were now ushered over to our "forming" DI.

This fella was about five foot nine, black and beefy. What were they feeding these guys? His cammies were flawless and shined from all the starch he used to press them with an iron. The forming DI was the DI that was in charge of teaching us the basics over the next few days, before we were handed over to our actual training DIs. Under his instruction, we were taught basic marching, customs, and regulations. He was also charged with getting all of the paperwork, medical shots, and various things we were required to have out of the way before Training Day One. We were even issued our rifles, at which point we had a brief moment to meet with our future senior DI.

Circling back to the medical shots, something happened there. I thought it was utterly ridiculous, but hilarious when I recall it, as I am sure most Marines do. The penicillin shot. We were given about a thousand various vaccines and other experimental shit the government felt we required, by Filipino Navy corpsmen (the docs). But the most important shot, given last, is the penicillin, otherwise known as the "magic meatball in the butt cheek" shot.

This painful experience began when the docs, who were laughing and talking Filipino the whole time, made us pull down our britches and shot it into our butt cheeks. It was administered through this device that resembled a pneumatic tool. The medication clumped up in the butt. So, we were sat down in a line, Indian-style, told to lock arms with the recruits in front of us and rock back and forth.

It was a ridiculous sight. The DIs were sitting around, having a blast, making us sing "Row Row Row Your Boat." Beyond the humility I learned that day, it was so painful I had a hard time sitting the next two days. Better than that, one idiot lied and said he wasn't allergic to penicillin so he would not be rejected.

I remember on the last day of forming that Rick and I thought this was not so bad at all. In fact, we thought this was going to be a cakewalk. What was everyone talking about? It had seemed more like propaganda the further along we got. When I was that young and ignorant to the rest of the world, I did not know any better. Then came the day we were handed over to our training DIs. Rick and I were officially baptized into Third Battalion, India Company, Platoon 3069.

We were on the second floor of the barracks with platoon 3068 below and 3070 above. Our company consisted of a lead and follow series, each having three platoons. The lead series were 3065, 3066, and 3067. If you haven't figured it out, it is done by numerical order. The beauty of our barracks was that it was right in front of a sand pit, or, as we called it, "the pit."

The pit was the cause of much disdain for us, as it was a discipline tool. The DIs would use it whenever they had a chance, for reasons of bad behavior, group punishment, or, on the days when they just wanted to plain old fuck with us, "recreational activities." Just for our convenience, the builders of Parris Island were kind enough to put these pits pretty much everywhere on the island. I never got a chance to thank them. Lest I not forget the horrible sand fleas that burrow into it.

I remember watching *Full Metal Jacket* religiously before boot camp and thinking how big the squad bays were in the movie. I can tell you now they were half that size. So, we were paraded into the squad bay and up to the quarter deck, which is the space that did not have any bunks. It, too, became another "recreational" area for the DIs. Believe me when I tell you the cement floor was as uncomfortable as it was cold and hard.

We were sat down in front of four DIs; one wore a black belt and three wore green ones. The company commanding officer, Captain Stermi, came in and gave us a little meet and greet. I never understood how a man that was five-foot-four could ever have been in Force Recon. I was starting to get bored, as I was unimpressed with the whole experience thus far. I looked over at Rick and silently mouthed, "What is this shit?"

He shrugged, and my attention went back to the DIs. At this point, they were taking some DI oath before us, which I did not understand nor did I care. The New Jersey punk in me was starting to come out. Drill instructors, all sergeants—Glenhamp, Whitehed, Truz, and Senior Drill Instructor Sergeant Woolridge—all swore to uphold the oath. Then came the order from the senior DI, or senior. "Drill instructors, instruct the recruits."

Rick and I looked at each other, surprised, and had zero time to comprehend what they were talking about before it came: hell. I can't really describe the havoc that followed in further detail, but I can say that it woke me the fuck up. Every Marine in existence knows what I am talking about, and I would not be doing justice to the future Marines by telling you. It's part of the brotherhood, the induction. All I can tell you is that pain was there, and it followed every minute of that day. Marine Corps boot camp in 1995 consisted of three phases. Each phase had its purpose, but I did not learn it until I finished them. At last, we were now in first phase.

Phase I was roughly four weeks in duration. This was effectively where discipline was forced onto us recruits by disorienting the hell out of us, and effectively cutting us off from our civilian habits and mindsets; they break you down. They also reinforce the mental and physical standards needed to perform under stressful situations, which would be simulated in the ensuing two phases. The primary focus was to give us some experience in combat situations by making us perform the most grueling activities the purpose of which we never understood.

We were required to learn and consistently use only the language and jargon peculiar to the Marine Corps. Make no mistake, we were recruits; worse than dirt. God help me if I had said, "I." The DIs would hone in on me and destroy me until I acknowledged I was "this recruit." They couldn't pronounce my last name correctly, so they called me all sorts of fun names, like, "Behey, Behzy, Betze, Bahezy, or Bitch," until they finally settled on "Beeznuts." It doesn't get much manlier than that nickname.

Phase I also taught me humility and instant willingness to follow orders. The DIs found out quickly that I needed extra conditioning, because I thought myself to be the ultimate bad-ass and quick with a joke. I had thought I was iron-thick. This extra attention was daily, and I found myself in both the pit and the quarter deck. Hell, it would be two to three times a day outside of the platoon "recreational activities." Rick even backed off from talking to me for a bit, because he was normally brought along to participate, and he couldn't take it anymore.

Some thought me a sick bastard, because I did have fun with it. I learned early on that everything was part of the game of molding. When called upon in the morning after reveille, I was immediately instructed to report to the quarter deck to perform my conditioning. I was now becoming so conditioned that the punitive actions implemented by the DIs were losing their effect. However, never underestimate the power of creativity of the Marine Corps drill instructor. These bastards were created to cause misery and invoke pain at a level I will never reach but will always envy.

Today was the same as the others before it. Conversely, Sergeant Whitehed had something new up his sleeve. The six of us that were being disciplined were told to "watch TV." To "watch TV," I had to get down in the push-up position and lift my torso off the ground, placing the weight on my elbows. It begins to hurt the elbows and your core section begins to burn. While balancing our weight in this position, we were ordered to "change the channel."

"Changing the channel" meant that we had to raise one arm and pretend to turn the knob of our imaginary television. That shit hurts. However, I, too, can play, for I discovered a loophole. When Sergeant Whitehed walked over and saw me with both elbows on the deck and my right hand thrusting forward, he had to ask.

"Recruit Beeznuts, what in the flying fuck are you doing? I told you to change the channel!" he bellowed.

I responded with the utmost sincerity, "Sir, this recruit's remote control does not seem to be working and will not change the channel."

I couldn't help but smirk at the cleverness of my response, and I had figured they had already beaten my ass so much that anything coming to me after this would be inconsequential. Sergeant Whitehed looked at me and was revving up to lay into me, but stopped suddenly. I looked up to see what stopped him, and noticed he was turning bright red. Three times Sergeant Whitehed tried to compose himself but stopped to catch his breath. Ultimately, he stood up straight and said, "As you were," and then headed to the DI shack and slammed the door.

All of us on the quarter deck started laughing softly, as it was damn funny. Then, the craziest thing happened. A shrieking laugh came from the shack and echoed throughout the squad bay. I likened it to a hyena calling out. Could it be? I just made an impenetrable DI laugh? An answer I would soon have, as the shack door opened and out he came.

His face was beginning to regain color as the blood drained from it. A few restrained chuckles escaped his lips as he adjusted his cammies and campaign hat back into perfect form. It was then that he regained his stoicism, slowly looked up, and locked eyes with me. He was now pissed off, and I really did not have a good feeling about it.

Sergeant Whitehed walked over to me, grabbed me by the blouse with one hand, and threw me up against the wall as if I had been a piece of paper; no bullshit. It had knocked the wind out of me. I had never been manhandled like that before. I don't recall the whole conversation, but I do remember him throwing his right finger in my face as he screamed at me.

The finger kept slamming into my cheekbone, and eventually he poked my left eye. Pain. Horrible pain. But I did not flinch or wince. I only closed the one eyelid so that the tears from the injury would not continue down my face. Most importantly, I stood there, taking my deserved reprimand. He wiped off my face the uncontrolled tears pouring from my injured eye and said, "No shame, son. Shake it off." I did, and this was how I gained Sergeant Whitehed's respect.

Moving on.

In the beginning of Phase II, or week five, which I always thought to be a break in the madness, and based on our performance of the weeks prior, we had to do either mess or maintenance duty, and this pertained to both series. In follow series, we were given maintenance duty, because we kicked ass in everything up to that point; fuck mess duty. Anyone who has done mess duty can tell you it was the worst. Maintenance, at least the part that Rick and I were assigned, consisted of helping supply organize their warehouse. It was a bit of fun, I will admit.

The primary focus of Phase II involves an introduction to field skills and includes two weeks of marksmanship training: a "grass week" and a qualifying week. These two weeks are spent in a class setting to learn about marksmanship principles of the M-16A2 and how to shoot it efficiently. The last week of Phase II is qualification of the M-16A2 at the two hundred–, three hundred–, and five hundred–yard line.

When I was pulling targets, or "butts," I got in trouble with quite a few of the many different DIs walking around down there, because there was this beautiful female DI. When I saw her, my jaw dropped. Seriously, she was hot and had these bright blue eyes. I was caught looking at her by another male DI. Immediately, he pointed it out and grabbed me right then and there and destroyed me. Luckily, this was during a cease-fire and there were no rounds coming down the range. Although the rage in his voice sounded like he didn't care one way or another.

He kept asking if I thought she was pretty, and I kept responding, "Yes, sir!" He motioned to his buddies to come and join in on the fun. Three of these male bastards kept at me for at least ten minutes. Finally, as a last-ditch effort to completely grind me into dirt, they called her over. Oh, fun. She commenced to destroy me by calisthenics after they explained the situation. She kept asking if I thought she was still pretty, to which I always responded, "Yes, ma'am!" The final time she asked, she made me stand up and looked me dead in the eye.

"You still think I am pretty?" she asked about an inch away from my face and with an evil look.

"There is no amount of pain that is going to make This recruit think you don't look magical, ma'am."

Boom! Charm bomb delivered. She stepped back and stared at me with a puzzled look. I believe a lesser man would have folded. "Get the fuck out of here, you disgusting recruit!" she screamed.

I went back up on the platform to pull the targets—out of breath, of course—and she was discussing the torture session with the other DIs. I watched them chuckle, amused. What a great networking event! I started to resent the woman. However, as she began to walk back to the Fourth Battalion (females) side of the range, she threw me a quick glance and smirked approvingly. I immediately perked up and went about my day with a small victory. Rifle qualification day was tomorrow and I was going to nail it.

I excelled at operating the M-16A2 rifle and I even had the range high score coming off the line with an "expert" rating. Rick qualified as an "expert" as well, but we agreed that the "sharpshooter" rifle badge, which was a level below expert, looked more prominent. I remember the DIs giving shit to the rest of the country bumpkins in our platoon for not doing a better job in qualifying than us city slickers. No matter now, the coveted Phase III was right around the corner.

Phase III was basically the "polishing up" of us recruits. This was where we honed our skills, knowledge, and were tested. It began with the A-line, where we learned to use our rifle under more realistic combat conditions, including firing at moving targets and from various combat stances rather than the positions used during Phase II. The biggest part of this phase is BWT, or basic warrior training.

Ah, BWT. This had to be my favorite part of boot camp. It lasted seven days and was the final hurdle of recruit training. This is where we learned the fundamentals of combat, sleeping in the field, and eating MREs. We lived in the field 24/7, for the duration, and it never stopped. Many of the skills we were taught included camouflage, low crawling, day and night land navigation, basic squad tactics, explosives, and other foundations of military prowess, including the gas chamber. Nowadays, the recruits call it "the crucible," which only lasts three days. Bitch, please.

The gas chamber is a cinderblock structure that was filled with tear gas. Every recruit will experience what it is like to breathe it in and how to cope when you do. When you do, you never forget it. All of the mucus in your body is evacuated through your nose and mouth. Not to mention, it burns like hell wherever you were exposed, especially your eyes. However, I did find that I breathed much better afterwards.

I remember our final BWT testing that consisted of the thousand-yard course. It was warm all week, and the weather was bearable. No sand fleas were bothering us, so it was a good time. That night, however, it rained like hell, and the temperature dropped to 37 degrees and windy. This was like a damn Greek tragedy. Still, we had to endure this damn course, which was now flooded with water, 37-degree water

As we lined up to take our turn, I felt as if we were awaiting our executions. One by one, I watched recruit after recruit duck-crawl through the cement cylinder and leap into the beginning of the five hundred yards of water. That was terrible. I thought I would be smart and hit the side of the bank where there was reprieve from the water. Nope. A DI immediately zeroed in on me and made me jump into the water twice, just so he was sure I was "nice and toasty."

I was forced to low-crawl through that first five hundred yards of water with explosions going off all around me. It felt like I was being stabbed all over my body with the intense cold water. Next, I got to turn over and fast-crawl through the water, with the wind bearing down upon me. When I reached the halfway point, I could not get the blank firing adaptor off of my M-16A2, because my fingers were frozen and I was damn near hypothermia. I could not feel my feet, either. A DI came over and took it off and screamed at me to get moving so I could get the blood back into circulation.

After I finished the hellish course, I was told to run back to the starting point with all of the others who had finished. You have to understand that this course was next to the old Vietnam air strips that were now decommissioned. Soaking wet, we had to run down the runway with the wind blowing on us for another thousand yards. That fucking day just wouldn't stop getting better.

I finally reached the change tent, where I was allowed to change into dry cammies and boots. Others were not as lucky; as I found out, a few did get hypothermia. It was a miracle I was not afflicted. To this day, I wonder how I did not get it.

After I finally warmed up and had some time to catch my breath as we waited for the others to finish, I decided I would write Maureen a letter. It was going well, and I was writing about what just transpired. However, the last line I was able to write said that I wasn't doing anything at that moment. Unbeknownst to me, a lead series DI had read that over my shoulder and started screaming at me. "You're not doing anything right now??? HUH?!?! Well, let's give you something to do!" he screamed.

He and about four other DIs came over to punish me. My name had become famous with the DIs in both series by that time, because of my smart-ass mouth, and so, a full-blown creativity session commenced. The DIs asked me what I thought was my favorite animal. At the time, I was not sure where this was going. I just muttered the first one that came to mind: tiger.

Again, foot in mouth. They made me walk on all fours like a tiger, and growl like one, too. This may not sound like a big deal, but doing that in the woods of Parris Island with all those damn pinecones makes it painful. I spent about an hour of running around on my hands and knees, growling, rolling on my back like a cat, and they forced me to scare other DIs and recruits as a tiger. Suffice it to say, that letter was never sent. They won this round.

After the week was finally over, we returned to our garrison for the final two weeks of recruit training. Final uniform inspection and drill competition was conducted by the base commanding general and bills had to be paid. What was that I just said? Bills had to be paid? Nobody told me or Rick about having bills while enduring this bullshit for twelve weeks. That's right, we paid for everything. Every civilian I have talked to thought we got a free ride. And yes, we do pay taxes on our salary.

When I was given my final bill from my senior DI, I looked dumbfounded. I remember him saying that the Marine Corps would give you everything you need. I came to find out that not only was I paying for everything I had been issued—like uniforms, paper, toiletries, and so forth—but I was also responsible for those awfully painful haircuts. You have to pay it in order to graduate. I was beyond annoyed. It was this annoyance that prompted me to ask my senior DI this question: "Sir, if the Marine Corps is going to give us everything we need, then why the hell am I paying my money for it?" I don't recall the answer he gave, because all four of the DIs teamed up on me and death shortly followed; nothing new at this point.

I considered this punishment a going-away present and one that I enjoyed, because, honestly, I was going to miss the bastards. You hate them when you start, but you love them when you leave. They become the fathers you never had. Again, they are revered and you never, ever forget their names as long as you live.

Graduation day is the day you realize it's over. This was Friday, February 16, 1996. There was a part of me that did not want to leave, and when I did, I got an idea of just how small was this island we had been on. Damn those bus drivers.

It turned out, they drive around the island to disorient you and make you think the place is huge. We did not have Google Earth back then to tell us otherwise. It was ridiculous. From the main parade deck to the main entrance gate was no longer than about three miles. That becomes the first disappointment in your enlistment.

Suffice it to say, I had the best experience of my life, and I learned that I could do things I once thought were impossible. By far, this was the single most important, proud moment of my life, and still is to this day. This day marks my transition from "I can't" to "I will." No longer was I the punk-ass kid from New Brunswick, New Jersey. I was now the man, the myth, the legend, the United States Marine.

As the universe would have it, Maureen was not able to come to the Friday graduation, because she was in Ireland for a field hockey program. Amidst much protest and almost shelling out over $1,200 for a plane ticket to come, her parents—most of all, her mother— were not going to allow her to skip out on that so she could see me for a day. After all this time, Rick's mom still resented the hell out of me. I did not care, for this was my day, my weekend, and my accomplishment. Rick and I were headed to the School of Infantry at Camp Geiger in North Carolina come Monday, because we forwent our ten-day leave. Rick's parents were giving us a ride up there.

This, this was when it started to get really interesting.

chapter seven

IN THE FMF

I am not going to bore you with the details of our military training up until being stationed at Camp Pendleton, California, but I can tell you it took Rick and me a total of nine months from boot camp till graduation from Recon School before we got there. We were given a choice of East Coast or West Coast, and knowing what life was like in Jacksonville, North Carolina, after School of Infantry, we both opted for the West Coast.

California . . . When we finished all of our military schools, including Recon School at Pendleton, Rick and I were given our permanent duty assignments. Again, we would be stationed together. We were assigned to First Reconnaissance Battalion at 33 Area, Camp Margarita (Margaritaville), Camp Pendleton, California. Long address.

Rick and I only knew California from the movies and the entertainment shows we used to watch, like *Hard Copy* and *Entertainment Tonight*. Since we were also both really into movies, this had a bit of sentiment for us. However, the reality was very different.

Visiting California is not the same as living there. Living there is like being in a bubble of surrealism. There is no humidity, it's always sunny, never snows unless you are up in the mountains, and the people are pretty laid back but extremely superficial. At least in New Jersey the people are open about their superficiality. Matter of fact, they normally tell you as much to your face. In California, you could be dead for three days before anyone knew it only because they came over to your house and only because they needed something, like a cup of sugar. I am nevertheless overlooking the most important thing I found fascinating: the women.

Anyone from Jersey can tell you New Jersey women want to be approached or pursued, and there is a game to be played in order to do so. That's why we say, "Bring your A-game." I had a problem with this when I was younger, because people would just tell me to go talk to the girl. Well, when you are thirteen, it's hard to have an A-game and furthermore, what the hell was I going to speak to her about? Nintendo? Skateboarding? New Kids on the Block? Hell, no! It can be nerve-wracking.

Anyway, I started, and by the time I was fifteen, I had mastered the craft of schmoozing women. Rick was always amazed by my abilities. Yes, I was attractive, and women always told me I was easy on the eyes, but it's not that I am all that, believe me. It was that my confidence was through the roof and I just knew what to say, when to say it, and how to say it. I learned not to give a shit what people thought of me, and it seemed to show. Rick was not as lucky.

Rick's sister was drop-dead gorgeous, but he was not so fortunate. Rick had blue eyes and pale skin with freckles. Don't get me wrong, I loved the guy, but he was not blessed with beauty. Still, even though he was relatively rough-looking, he carried himself well, and you couldn't help but pay attention to him: he stood out. At least that's what his girlfriends would tell me. Personally, I think he was rough-looking due to the fact that he had been in so many fights throughout his young life. However, women liked him a lot.

Back to California.

SOUNDTRACK: INXS, "Need You Tonight"

After we got settled in our Fleet Marine Force (FMF) duty station, we began to party. I'll never forget my first night out in San Diego. Rick and I went to a place called Moose McGillycuddy's in Pacific Beach, San Diego, at the urging of a fellow squad member. He informed us that this was the place to go to meet local and "interesting" women.

In retrospect, we lovingly called it "Mooses" for short. Let me just say: what a meet market! Rick and I had never seen a place like this before. We were used to places like Hunka Bunka, Deco, The Tunnel, Webster Hall, and Limelight. This was a fun bar with a dance floor, but nothing if anything, a place to get laid.

After Rick and I used our fake IDs to get past the bouncers, we entered the place. Jersey men must carry themselves differently, because everyone noticed us as we walked down to the bar area near the dance floor. When I ordered a beer, three different women turned their heads towards me. Rick and I were a little rattled.

Unbeknownst to me, it turned out, I had an accent of sorts when I spoke. I never noticed. This always prompted California women to talk to me out of sheer curiosity. The dialogue would always open with one of the same three questions: What exit are you from? Do you know anybody in the mafia? So, you're from Joisey?

Allow me to answer.

"What exit are you from?" You must be joking. Not for nothing, there's more to New Jersey than the New Jersey Turnpike or the Garden State Parkway. We do have plush greenery, beaches, asshole drivers on toll roads, cities, and attitude. Hell, they even call it the Garden State. There is food here like no other, and definitely pizza above everything else. If anything, they should call it the pizzeria state. People think we wear our exit number on our sleeve like a badge of courage in which we identify our clans. However, I'm from exit 9.

"Do you know anybody in the mafia?" I always responded by looking around cautiously, and asking, escalating from near-whispering to almost shouting, with every question, "Who's asking? Who do you work for? Who the fuck sent you?" Not for nothing, of course, we all know someone in the mafia. The state is in between Philadelphia and New York City, with tons of dockyards. Ya think?

"So, you're from Joisey?" Joisey? Joisey? What the hell is that? Nobody from New Jersey has ever said that, and we get really inflamed when asked that question. It's like someone dragging a fork slowly on a chalkboard. If you keep saying "Joisey," expect someone from Jersey to make a face as if you farted in an elevator. Yes, it bothers us that much.

So, those are the three questions I'm always asked at one time or another during the conversation. I have never had a poker face, so you will always know what I'm feeling as I'm feeling it. Whether it's disgust, anger, amusement, or pure lunacy, you'll see it. I tell you this now, because when I'm asked these questions, I don't hide my disgust for them.

Women are aggressive out there, and will come up

to you. Truth be told, I loved it. Rick was often in heaven, because it was very easy for him to score a date. Apparently, confidence was a turn-on for Cali women. Good for him, though.

There was always something to do in Cali. Rick and I got spoiled by all the dry weather. It was the only place I had lived where the people were accepting of tattoos in the 1990s. I had added a few, after thinking they were once taboo. They get addictive.

The sun was always out. The few times is wasn't, they called it "winter." Camping was always a blast. You could go on the beaches and park all year round without having to pay, like you do in Jersey. Then there was the surfing.

SOUNDTRACK: Incubus, "Wish You Were Here"

Surfing. Nature's way of soothing the savage beast. Never in my whole life have I ever been so at peace as I have when scoring a perfect ride. Anyone who has surfed knows what I am talking about. I liken it to a drug high, and I have done some crazy club drugs, except this drug is 100 percent natural, legal, and doesn't kill brain cells. I struggled the first few times out, but, thankfully, I am able to pick things up very quickly. That first real ride I caught was amazing.

Normally, the waves came in sets of three. I had been told to grab the last wave, but the first one was cresting perfectly and without any chop. I paddled like hell to get to the break point. Slowly, it picked me up from the bottom to the top of the crest and I thought I was going to bite it hard. All of a sudden, I crouched down a little, and my board shot down the wave to the left of the break. It took a second before I started to slalom along the wave. The sheer force of power of nature touched me in a way I had never felt before.

The ride lasted a good fifteen seconds, because the subsequent waves continued the momentum, and it felt like I was flying on a hoverboard. It was as if I was attuned with the Earth. I know, it sounds corny, but it's true. The entire experience has made me environmentally conscientious and somewhat earthly spiritual ever since.

Before I knew it, I had four different types of boards: egg, hybrid, short-board, fun-board. It becomes your life. You live it, breathe it, and talk about it constantly. I was continuously checking surf reports to make sure I was hitting the right beaches: Tamarack, Del Mar, Lower Trestles, Trestles, and so on.

While I surfed, Rick would hit on the local women. It worked out for both of us. Sadly, though, I would find out just how busy it was to be a Fleet Recon Marine. However, I surfed as much as I could. It gave me a sort of solace, a sense of humanity, and a penance for my work. Most importantly, my soul was always at ease. Since I have stopped, there's been a dark void there.

Anyway, back to Marine life.

The FMF: Fleet Marine Force. It is the goal of every Marine in the beginning of his journey. All of us who have made that foray into the halls of the insane tough, always strive to get to the Fleet Marine Force. The FMF is when you are no longer in training, and the Marine Corps sends you to combat any deterrence of American capitalism. Or some politicians' idea of peace through show of force.

Rick and I have been to so many shitholes on this planet that we've lost faith in humanity. The place where I started losing sleep was East Timor. That operation, Operation Stabilise, had caused me severe sleeping problems. My stress had built up over time, and without the ability to release it, I would never sleep well again, even less so now, after the Iraq invasion.

My former girlfriends were always scared to sleep next to me, because something new seemed to happen each night I stayed with them. Some even went as far as to call it "an adventure at home." There could be anything from screaming in my sleep to actual physical contact: punching, kicking, even sometimes choking them without realizing it.

Assholes with PhDs, who have never set foot in combat, call it "PTSD." In my opinion, it kept things interesting. Every one of these women would bring it to my attention, but I usually dismissed it. You won't matter in a month anyway, I would always think.

East Timor was a worthless shithole in Indonesia. It was some dismal Third World island nation at the end of the Indonesian Islands chain. In retrospect, there was no real purpose for our unit to even be there, which made it worse. It wasted a life of someone I knew for no reason other than politics. It hit me hard, because it was the first loss I had experienced under my command.

It was a hot August in 1999, and our unit was three hundred miles off the coast of Perth, Australia. I was looking forward to a much-deserved port stop, and even more to the Australian women. Those Australian women welcomed the U.S. Marines like conquering heroes, because the Australian men constantly treated their women like second-class citizens. After four months at sea, it was time for a little release. The Thirty-first Marine Expeditionary Unit (REIN), or MEU, was cruising along aboard the LHA-3, USS *Belleau Wood*, when the call came in to get routed to East Timor. Fucked again, the story of my life.

The mission sounded simple: laze the target for the bombers to take out the insurgents' communication tower; no commissioned officers required for this operation except on radio; and Rick was put on the extraction team that would pick us up. I was the team leader and given two teams totaling twelve men, because that was what the mission needed. But there is no such thing in the Marine Corps as a simple mission, and I knew better. We were off the record helping the Australians combat these little bastards in East Timor, so we needed to exercise caution in our involvement.

Military intelligence butchered it once again by briefing us that there might be some "light" resistance. As we came to find out once on the ground, 150 Indonesian soldiers were not "light" even if our unit was hardcore. Still, the mission went on, and there we were, in the East Timorese jungle. Objective Alpha was reached undetected, fire mission requested, and now was time to sit with the laser on the communications tower in the middle of the insurgents' camp.

There we sat for about five minutes, motionless, with more than my fair share of bugs crawling all over my face, some as large as my middle finger. To move would have compromised our position and the mission. It was the ultimate in discipline. Two minutes after calling in the fire mission, I heard the sound of crackling thunder, and then a loud boom reverberated through the air and ground. It was so close it even made me catch my breath. A magnificent plume arose from the devastation. Mission objective completed.

Now we needed to double-time it to Landing Zone

(LZ) Omega. As we began to head back to the LZ, I noticed the sound of breaking branches and the soft muttering of Indonesian lingo coming from behind my teams. I gave the hand signal to haul ass, because eighty-three—as it was later reported by infrared satellite imaging—insurgents were right behind us and closing in fast.

All thirteen of us began an all-out sprint as the gunfire erupted. The whizzing of the bullets was in my ears, but I was able to tune out the continuous sounds of the AK-47s, because I was focused. Get to the LZ, I kept telling myself, no matter what it takes. I was already enraged by MI's faulty intel. I ordered my squad not to engage unless it was absolutely necessary; it would take too much time we did not have. We were already compromised and needed immediate evacuation. The LZ lay just over the hill, but out in the open.

The enemy was gaining ground, and I needed to slow them down. As my two teams set up a defensive firing position that resembled a horseshoe, to cover all angles with the ocean to our backs, I gave the order to open fire. Leaves from the plants and palm trees fell down as the bullets ripped through the air. I fired a few grenades from my M203 into the tree line. It stopped the Indonesians for the moment and gave us enough of a chance to make them waste time on trying to figure out how many people they were up against. I could hear the sound of the CH-46 coming up from the rear. However, my radio operator relayed that the pilots could not set down there, because the LZ was too hot from enemy fire. Frustrated, I reluctantly gave the order to vacate to LZ Sigma.

LZ Sigma was two miles to the north and down a long dirt road, on foot. I gave my slack man, Lance Corporal (LCPL) Crooner, an order to set booby traps along the route. This was not to take out the enemy forces, but rather give the squad more time to reach the LZ. Claymores were the deterrent of choice for this task, and Crooner was on it. That guy was gifted with setting them up in a matter of seconds. Every two hundred feet, Crooner would lay two, adjacent but staggered. The fuse was a tension wire that would actuate the Claymore by tripping or stepping on the wire. In the past, it had been 100 percent effective.

I was about a hundred feet ahead and providing LCPL Crooner with cover fire. Crooner was on his last Claymore when I saw him fall backwards; he was hit. When a person gets hit with a round, typically it sounds like a thin bamboo rod smacking a hard, leather surface, shortly followed by a thud. The thud is usually the bullet, which travels slower than the speed of sound, entering its intended target. The spray of blood from impact is not how it looks in the movies: it's minimal at best. I had seen people shot plenty of times during my time in the Marines, but never like it was in the movies. It looked more like a trickle of blood coming from the wound, but the flow wouldn't stop. Twice Crooner was hit; once in the center chest and once in the lower-left abdomen.

I ran back to Crooner, who was now gasping for breath and starting to go into shock. I tried to drag him, but it was too slow, so I slung his rifle and him over my shoulders: firemen's carry. As I began running down the dirt road, two of my team members saw that Crooner was in need, and they rushed over to grab him. I refused their help. My responsibility, my Marine.

The first of the Claymores went off, which meant the enemy was less than a quarter of a mile away now and closing fast. Each time they set off a Claymore, they would slow down, but be back at it again moments later; tenacious little bastards.

I could see the CH-46 with the back door open. It had already been a mile and a half of running with Crooner on my shoulders. I continued to reassure myself, to ease the pain screaming from my legs. Blood now soaked my back from Crooner's wounds and his groaning became softer and softer. Stay with me, you little fuck, stay with me, I muttered.

After I passed my squad's defensive position, I ran up the rear ramp of the CH-46. I softly laid Crooner on the deck of the helicopter as the rest of the teams entered. My legs buckled from the pain, and I fell onto the troop seat. The helicopter took off as soon we received the all-clear.

The Claymores continued to go off on the ground, and clouds of dirt could be seen from the windows of the helicopter as Rick continued his steady suppressing fire with the door gunner. doc, began to work on Crooner. I just stayed there, kneeling next to him, holding his hand.

I cannot stress this enough: it is never as it is in the movies. I continued to think that over and over as I looked at Crooner lying there gasping for air. Blood was now coming out of his mouth, and his breathing was more strained. At this point, his entire torso was covered in blood. The worst part was that the blood was blackish-colored, meaning that his liver had been hit. This was not a wound from which you recover.

Crooner became aware of his condition when he looked at both the Doc and me, but not only that, blood was now beginning to choke his every breath. With his left hand, Crooner dug into his trouser pockets. Pulling out a picture of his family back in whatever state he was from, he handed it over to me.

"Tell them I . . . *(coughs, spits blood)* tell them I'm sorry. *(Coughs, coughs, spits a large amount of blood),*" Crooner said as he grabbed my hand. "Promise me . . ."

Just as soon as I nodded, Crooner went limp. His head rolled back, with his eyes open. After about three seconds of what seemed like eternity, I realized he was not blinking or breathing, and shook him. There was no reaction. Panicking, I shook Crooner a few more times before doc regretfully called the time of death. I began CPR, but doc tried to stop me. Pushing away his hand each time, I continued. My Marine, my responsibility, I thought, and I was not going to lose this one.

Doc had to jump up and physically restrain me. I tried to resist, and Rick with a few other members of my teams came to his aid. My face was turning red and the veins were popping out of my forehead as I fought hard to get back to reviving that boy, that twenty-year-old boy.

They could see I was hurting. It was the guilt and the inevitability of the situation. When I finally calmed down, I took a couple deep breaths and looked around the cabin. All my Marines were watching me with solemn expressions, as if to say, "We know you tried, boss, we know you did your best."

Rick came up to me and said through the internal comms, "It's the job. It's the job, man." Then he patted me on the shoulder and went back to door gunner area.

Doc let me go after I settled down. I threw down the tourniquets that he had been using to stop the bleeding as I stood up in utter disappointment. The teams left me to my thoughts as I slowly sat down at the front of the helicopter. They just sat there looking at the now-corpse of LCPL Crooner; a reminder of things that could happen to them. It became very real.

I looked back and could see the loss on their silent faces. They levied no blame towards me, because we all understood the risks. I shouldn't have let him lay so many fucking Claymores. Yet it was those Claymores that saved us. Another quandary that will haunt me for the rest of my days. Crooner would still be here if he hadn't done that last set, right? What if?

Skip ahead to his funeral. I was the flag presenter to LCPL Crooner's family. I was ordered to keep my mouth shut about the entire operation, as the Marines were officially there as advisors, not operators. Regardless, I felt the family had the right to know, and told them during the reception how it really happened. I thought it would give them closure, but instead I received a slap across the face from his mother. She tore at my uniform and cursed at me. She now blamed me for her loss, and I have never forgotten it. Stupid.

Eventually, Crooner's mother wrote to me to say she forgave me. It's an extremely hard thing to swallow, when a fellow Marine dies. It's like part of your soul dies with them every time it happens. This, not combat, is why so many of us commit suicide once we return back to the USA.

We feel that we let our brothers down. We feel that it was because of us that they died. There are no words, no sort of comfort to make it easier for us. Going to the VA hospital feels even worse, it feels like we did not give enough. But watching it happen before your own eyes brings you back into real life.

I still have that burden of guilt, and have never slept through the night since. It is not easy to "just let it go," as clueless civilians always tell me. Especially when you think you are the reason for the loss.

These are your brothers, through thick and thin, doing a job that only less than half of 1 percent of the entire population can do. The bond is intense, and I will never get over it. Even if I die, my spirit will guard their final resting place. We are that tight of a group. It's a hard, hard thing to move past losing one of your brothers.

And then came Iraq.

chapter eight

IN THE FMF: IRAQ

SOUNDTRACK: Soundgarden, "Burden in My Hands"

I never forget the culture shock of first arriving in Iraq. I remember bits and pieces, as they now flash through my mind like a montage. Flashes of shepherds walking their flocks of sheep in the street past their derelict mud huts, burning cars, the dilapidated buildings, and people staring at us with disgust from both sides of the roads. Also, there was the dust. It was everywhere. Couldn't get it out of my mouth or nose. My boogers had doubled in size while in this place.

Prior to the invasion, we were based out of Camp Matilda in Kuwait. It was nothing but desert as far as the eye could see. One could say it was endless beach. It also reminded me of CAX in Twentynine Palms, California. Nobody likes Twentynine Palms. Nobody. Although I suppose that getting off the USS *Nassau* (LHA-4) was a good thing at that point, since we had been on it for almost three months. I am sick of the Navy boats. I swear to God, I had done more time on naval vessels than a lot of first-enlistment Navy personnel.

At any rate, this was the real deal. Rick and I had been on plenty of missions together, but never the scope of this one. The entire First Reconnaissance Battalion was engaged. We did our typical safety briefs, which I always found ridiculous, given the circumstances. One must be safe when killing the enemy with projectiles and explosives, I guess. Then essential personnel—staff sergeants and above—were briefed on the mission objectives. Rick and I had just been freshly promoted to the rank of staff sergeant at the beginning of the month, so this was our first "I am important enough to attend" brief.

Our first objective was to head north and join up with the Royals (British Royal Marines) in the city of Basra. Our company commander, Captain Kersey, was pulled to assist with forward operations regarding Baghdad. We were to eventually meet up with him and a first lieutenant, whose name I, regrettably, do not remember. He was a good guy, but Rick and I weren't with him long enough to remember his name. Simply put, his name was the Lieutenant.

Upon our arrival, we met up with the Royals and were soon engaged by small insurgencies. However, HQ thought it was more pertinent for our company to move north to Nasiriyah and Gharraf, and let the Royals be the lead on Basra. I heard that Basra was quite the battle for them, too. I loved those Limey bastards.

We were engaged numerous times while we fought our way through Nasiriyah. We sustained very few casualties when we took the city. It was the same for Gharraf. However, the main goal was Baghdad, which was 117 miles northwest. This is where we would expect the bulk of the casualties to occur. As with all forward operations, we had some downtime prior to the big push for Baghdad. We took ours in a big and empty building that looked like a warehouse at one time.

I remember sitting on a wooden ammo crate, which also made a great toilet seat, and playing cards with Rick and Sergeant Jamal White, all the while listening to Linkin Park's "Somewhere I Belong" on a boom box. I don't recall how we appropriated the boom box, but sometimes it's just better to not ask.

Sergeant White was a beefy, six-foot-one black guy from the Bronx. I sometimes called him "Denzel," because he walked just like Denzel Washington. He was tough as nails, but funny as hell. Naturally, he fit in with us. He, Rick, and I were a tight group.

Never give Marines downtime. When Marines have downtime, stupid shit happens. Don't believe me? Google "marines with downtime funny." All I know is that I never thought it was possible to joust with mops and bicycles. I digress. As always, we were talking about randomly insignificant stuff. Today's conversation revolved around "What animal would you like to be reincarnated as?"

I said tiger, because it was already near and dear to me. Furthermore, polite by nature unless disrespected, and they are the top of their food chain. Typical of Jamal, he picked gorilla, because he liked pounding his chest and scaring white people. Yeah, sick humor, but we laughed anyway. Finally, there was Rick. He picked a raven.

"A raven? Why the fuck would you pick a raven?" I asked, bemused.

"Because ravens are bad-ass. Nobody messes with them, and they don't give a rat's shit about nothing or nobody. That Poe guy did a cool-ass poem about them, too. They even have their own color. They're not black-colored, they're raven-colored. Beyond that, I think they transport the soul when you die. They carry you onto the next plain. Just an all-around bad-ass bird. You gotta respect them," he explained while throwing down another card.

"You just like black shit, don't you, Calderra?" Jamal joked.

"You put way too much thought into this, I think," I said.

"Whatever, bitches. If I die and you see a raven laughing at you, that'll be me," Rick said.

As we were just about to dissect this further, the Lieutenant came over and said, "Staff sergeants Calderra and Beeznuts, I need you to come with me right now. You are going to be heading to the forward area to meet up with Captain Kersey. The CO wants to brief you immediately. Sergeant White, I need you to stand by with your team."

We grabbed our gear, then Rick and I followed the Lieutenant over to a briefing area with the battalion commanding officer, Lieutenant Colonel Quinn. As he entered the area, we came to attention. He ordered us at ease and began the brief.

Apparently, while Captain Kersey was doing reconnaissance of the proposed invasion area in southern Baghdad, the fighting became pretty fierce. We believed it was because Captain Kersey's outfit was a small element, much easier to engage. The reason we were requisitioned was because the two platoon squad leaders were hit and taken out of action. Needless to say, the injuries were severe enough to undergo field surgery, and one of them had a 50-50 chance while the other was stable.

Normally, our new rank would make us the "unit leaders" for the entire platoons. However, expertise and experience in the squad leader position were the priority for this mission. Lieutenant Colonel Quinn then told us that Captain Kersey had specifically requested both Rick and me as replacements for the time being, as the mission was essential to the follow element (units coming up from the rear). We were to be delivered via free fall, para-dropped from a C-130 into Hor Rajab, which is on the southern border of Baghdad, and link up with Captain Kersey and Bravo Platoon.

Let me be very clear. I hate jumping out of planes, especially free fall. I used to enjoy roller coasters, but jump school and various missions have since taken that joy away. The only way I was able to force myself to jump out of an airplane was to make myself commit to death. What I mean is, I had to accept that I would die. It probably sounds sick, but that way I removed the fear of death, which influenced my fear of heights. Remove the fear, and you become invincible. Plus, you are placing complete trust in the person who packed your chute. Hopefully, they weren't hungover from the night before. Oh, the extra pay we get is amazing, too. Last I checked, being scuba- and jump-qualified scored me an extra $150 a month.

We got some sleep, because this was going to be a day insert, and neither of us felt nervous. I asked that we also forgo the HALO drop, which normally begins at 15,000 feet. I wanted to jump from about 12,000 feet for this op, and I didn't feel like wearing a mask to jump; just more crap to carry. The recommended hard deck for us was 6,000 feet to deploy chutes. I was never one for being a sitting duck, as it was possible that the enemy would be firing up at us, so I was planning to deploy under 4,500 feet. There are hard decks for a reason, folks, and I'll get to that part.

When the next morning came—0930, to be precise—

we were put on the C-130. The crew chief gave us the usual "I am the commander of this area" speech. This oration is about how he controls everything in the fuselage of the aircraft, and we had to listen to everything he said or he would throw us off the plane—which we were jumping out of already.

Anyway, the plane then took off towards Baghdad. I think we were at max altitude in a matter of minutes. We were in the air for about forty-five minutes before we were over our landing zone. It was at this time that the crew chief signaled us for pre-jump check.

SOUNDTRACK: White Zombie, "Super Charger Heaven"

White Zombie was for when I jumped. Hey, it put me at ease, and that song particularly got my adrenaline pumping, especially the beginning of it. As the back of the plane slowly opened up and the sun shone across the Iraqi horizon, Rick looked over at me and held up six fingers, which meant 6,000 feet. He did so twice. I acknowledged with a middle finger. He gave me a lot of shit about not wanting to pull at 6,000, but I promised I would this time.

The crew chief counted down from three on his hand and gave us the go-ahead. I pushed play on my Walkman and jogged off the back of the plane. As soon as I left the rear ramp ledge, that gut sensation hit me. God, I hated it. It took a good three seconds for me to open my eyes and get over it. Just so you know, that's one Mississippi, two Mississippi, three Mississippi . . .

Finally, I opened my eyes, relaxed, and got into freefall formation with Rick. I could see the landing zone below us, with our new platoon, as they let off a smoke grenade to mark the landing. They looked like ants.

However, 6,000 feet came fast on the altimeter, and Rick gave the signal to pull. He went first, and then I pulled my actuation device. Normally, the chute deploys in about three seconds, tops, but this took far longer. I looked up, and the A-lines to the ram-air canopy were tangled in a knot that would not allow the chute to fully deploy. In this type of situation, most people would have flipped out. I was able to stay calm, because I had 5,000 more feet—or so I thought.

It was clear that I was not going to be able to undo the knot, so I released the chute and began free fall again. I was now at 2,000 feet, and the ground was fast approaching. Now I was feeling a smidgen of anxiety. I was able to get my reserve chute to open at 500 feet and finally slow my decent at 300 feet. But I realized that I was coming in too fast, and that a regular landing would not suffice. Emergency landings like this required that I come in and skid across the ground, a sort of sliding into second base and rolling until stop. Lucky for me, there was a lot of sand.

Regardless, I assessed that I would also have to release the back-up chute just as I came in, so that I wouldn't get tangled in the lines and snap my neck; tricky. The platoon was watching this unfold on the ground as I drew closer to them. Some of the bastards were already making bets to see if I would make it or not.

I aimed my descent path towards them and was now at 100 feet and still coming in too fast. This is some scary shit, believe me. As I lined up to the platoon directly ahead, I could see my shadow getting closer by the second. As I glided quickly, I pulled down on the steering cords. The problem with the sand is the sun's reflection. The sun was so bright that I was having a hard time gauging my final height.

After hitting what seemed to be the eight-foot mark, I released the chute and slammed into the ground, skidding and rolling, at about seven miles per hour. To add insult to injury, the final stretch of skidding happened on my stomach and partially my face. That was an awesome twenty-foot skid that rubbed my nipples raw. Not the cleanest landing I have ever done, but nonetheless, I could walk away from it.

As I lay there for a second to regain my composure and dignity while spitting out the sand in my mouth, I said to myself, "I have arrived."

I could hear Rick calling me a "dumb shit" from the air as he touched down like a feather. The platoon was clapping and whistling as well. As I looked up and started to dust myself off, Captain Kersey walked up and stood over me, blocking the sun from my eyes.

"I am beginning to think we need to change your name to Murphy's Law. I trust you didn't get any sand in your clit, did you, staff sergeant?" he asked firmly.

"No, sir. Good to see you too, sir," I responded.

"Well then, get your fancy ass up, dust off, and take five. Then you two get your asses on the back of that five-ton. I'll brief you both on the way."

"Aye, sir," Rick and I responded.

As we rolled out, Captain Kersey explained that the objective was to secure a building in the heart of the southern tip of Baghdad for HQ operations, which would demoralize the enemy, while most of the U.S. units moved north into Baghdad. This meant that we were securing the area for other Marine units to come through from the south. It was going to be the strategic stronghold in all of the southern sector of Baghdad.

I would tell you the name of the area, but I can't pronounce the name, nor did I care enough to learn how to. I used to sound like I was clearing my throat when I was attempting to speak Arabic. I tried to make an attempt so that I did not infuriate the locals, in an effort to keep more of them from joining the insurgents.

After a bit of time, we arrived at the forward area. To my surprise, Baghdad was huge. It looked nothing like I had envisioned. I had seen the "Swords of Qadisiya" on television, during the Persian Gulf War, but nothing prepares you for the actual thing in person. The fast movers had done their job bombing with pinpoint accuracy, because the place looked like Detroit. However, I was told it didn't change much from before the bombings, more of an improvement.

We dismounted the five-ton and mustered into our respective squads. To get to the area where we were to start the breeching so we could secure the proposed HQ operations building, we had to patrol down a road with eight-foot-tall walls. If the situation wasn't stressful enough already, they had to add these walls to the mix. Hajis had a bad habit of hiding at the top and conducting ambushes. Well, if you want to call them ambushes. They were more like they were peeking over the top and firing an AK-47. Normally, they missed by a couple of feet. However, every time we thought we heard movement, we would get a little spooked because nobody wanted to be "that guy." Not fun.

Now we had the fun task of breeching these shithole shacks beyond the walls along the roadway, to assure that the convoy with all the supplies was able to move forward. In an effort to save time, we were going to do door-to-door breeching in teams of two. I was stuck with one of my fire team leaders, Corporal LaFaire.

As we began down the street, I took notice of the ramshackle area. Remnants of cars were on fire. Bodies and body parts were strewn here and there, but that wasn't caused by us. These people were killed by the insurgents that wanted to strike fear into those who thought about coming to our aid.

Women, men, boys, and girls were scattered everywhere. I'm not going to go into more detail, except that it was pretty horrific and these images stay with you the rest of your life. You get the idea: the place was a mess. To a normal person, this was beyond tolerable, but I did not have the option to object openly. I had to endure, and I could not allow feelings to get the better of me, to cloud my judgment. My views on humans as a species have suffered severely since.

A few of the new guys were getting sick to their stomachs. I guess they were still able to be human. As a staff sergeant, I had to maintain discipline, but it does wear on you. However, the only thing that made me physically sick was the smell. If it wasn't the burning corpses, it was the ones that were rotting in the sun. What a putrid smell. It smelled like sour, rotten eggs with a touch of ammonia, and burning hair. Needless to say, I wanted to get my squad through there as fast as possible.

First Platoon, which was ours, and Second Platoon both headed west down the street on opposite sides, towards the T-handle five hundred yards away. We took the right side while Second took the left. Third Platoon was coming up from the south to link up with us at the T-handle. This was so we could head north, up the road, to where it split into a V, and establish that building there as an HQ for the main invasion. We moved along and finally came to the section that we were to begin breeching. Just as we did in training, we began kicking in the doors, securing the room, and keeping an eye out for snipers.

It was going well. When I say well, I am being a little cavalier. Anyone who tells you that running into a room by yourself, blind, is fun and exciting is normally an unsafe and unbalanced person. It is not a good time, and definitely not fun for the whole family. Alas, Corporal LaFaire was complaining about having to take a piss. Due to the stress, I am sure. I told him to go in the small alley while I went next door and decided to clear it all by myself. There is a reason why rules are in place. As I say to this day, "Common sense is not a common virtue."

I kicked in the door, which opened to the right, walked in with my rifle at the ready, and quickly surveyed the area. It wasn't much of a room. There was a table in the middle of it, with two stools and some silverware, a few shelves, and what looked like a dirty mattress on the ground in the back. I thought there was nothing to it, so I relaxed and dropped down my rifle, ready to check on the next room. Unbeknownst to me, there was a Haji hiding in the area behind the door. Apparently, the little bastard didn't know we were coming.

As I began to walk towards the front door, he flew out from behind it and leapt onto my back, completely surprising me. From behind, he was able to wrap his legs around my waist like a backpack and get me in a choke hold in seconds. In retrospect, it was kind of embarrassing, because he was a little guy, maybe 140 pounds, tops. However, he had gotten the drop on me, and I could not raise my rifle because the tactical sling allowed him to keep it pressed against my body while choking me. I couldn't yell for help, either, because my vocal cords were restricted.

My other option was to stab the motherfucker with

my K-bar, but, again, it was unreachable. I don't know where he learned this technique, but it was very effective. Because my adrenaline kicked in, it was hard to breathe, so every time I exhaled, he would clamp down harder. No matter how many times I backed up and slammed him into the wall, he stayed attached. I could not break his grip with my hands, either.

As I started to lose consciousness, I tried to shake him loose one last time. This was the first time in my life I really thought I was going to die. It wasn't dying that bothered me; it was losing. Sounds crazy, but Marines don't like losing even in the face of death. We believe it's better to die on our feet than on our knees, and this was that moment.

I ran over to the table and grabbed the first sharp item I could get. It happened to be a fork. I spun around and fell backwards on top of the table so that I could pin him on it. I started stabbing the Haji in his right leg, over and over. It was the last thrust into his leg that caused him to let go, because I started twisting the fork in his flesh. He let out a cry and finally let go just as I was about to black out.

He ran out of the room, limping, and ran to the right, towards the T-handle. To this day, I am absolutely amazed that not one Marine engaged him. Everyone was oblivious. Good job, guys!

I collapsed to my knees and gasped for air, catching my breath. Even in my weakened state, I stumbled to my feet and drew out my Berretta M9 with full intention of lighting that bastard up with full metal–jacketed lead. As I staggered out to the street, I watched him round the corner into obscurity. Sadly, he got away. To this day, I have problems entering rooms without getting a little twitchy.

Corporal LaFaire came up from behind, and, feeling somewhat hazy, I swung around my pistol and struck him on his Kevlar helmet. It took him a second to shake it off, and he saw the bruising on my neck. Oh, what an ass-chewing I gave him about the length of time it should take to piss!

Rick ran over and asked if I was okay. I briefed him, and he laughed. As mad as I was at the time, I, too, began to laugh, because that was all I could do. Got to love that sick Marine sense of humor. What a fucking day already, seriously. I should have checked behind the door. What if?

As I regained my composure for the second time that day, I again started down the right side of the street, making sure that Corporal LaFaire went in first every time. If we were back at Pendleton, I'd have him policing rocks at the barracks, but under the circumstances, I thought this was fitting. Son of a bitch must pay.

Second Platoon made it to the end of the street on their side, as we were slightly behind them on the right side. All of a sudden, I got a really bad feeling in my gut, like a sixth sense of sorts. As soon as that feeling came, shots rang out.

The first two Marines in Second Platoon, who were on point, went down. Our platoon halted, and I ran to the front of the line to get a better picture of the scenario, as Second Platoon began returning fire to the north diagonally from them. I was about to peer around the corner when bullets came raging towards my head from the south, hitting the corner of the building behind me. Luckily, I was able to retract fast enough to get out of their paths.

I called the radio operator up, so that I could inform

Third Platoon. It turned out that Third was held up as well by the same assholes ambushing us. I was able to grab a mirror from one of the secured rooms. It was bulky, but it did give me a chance to see around the corner with enough time to zero in on the targets. Then they shot my mirror to pieces. It vibrated in my hands when it shattered. Would you believe I got a glass splinter?

Diagonally to the south, three Hajis were firing out of the first-floor window in a three-story building, and they had RPGs. Directly in front of me to the west, at the end of the T-handle, was a staircase that presumably went to the roof of the building. This would give us the ability to take out the insurgents on the northern part of the street. However, to the north, there were two teams of Hajis on opposite sides of the street, also on the first floors, creating a wall of fire. They were laying it on heavy, too.

By this time, Captain Kersey and Rick had made it up to my position. I briefed them on what I saw and we began to organize a plan. As we were doing this, our oblivious radio operator decided he would peer around the corner to the north out of sheer curiosity. I turned around and saw the Haji team to the south, readying to fire an RPG at our position. I yelled out, "RPG!" and everyone scattered.

The radio operator was slow to process what was happening, and was not going to make it if he didn't move faster. I grabbed him by his radio pack and twisted to my right while jumping backwards. This guy had some guardian angels, because the impact was high and shrapnel barely missed him. I watched as the ground kicked up dust from the pieces. Unfortunately, I pulled two muscles in my lower back, and small pieces of shrapnel went into my right and left shins. Not to mention I now had this horrible ringing in my ears.

Rick ran over to me to make sure I was okay and helped me to my feet. Our corpsman, doc, immediately gave me 1,600 mg of Motrin to slow down the inflammation until I could get some ice on it. It was this injury that has led to my lower back problems ever since.

Rick was now pissed off at the situation, because he saw it unraveling if we didn't act soon. He ran to the southern corner and assessed the circumstances further. Captain Kersey could see the look in his eye.

"Calderra, you stay put!" Captain Kersey yelled.

"Sir, if we don't get on top of this now, we're going to be sitting ducks when their buddies arrive. If I can get to that fuckin' roof, I can at least take out those three fuckers on our right side of the northern side with a LAW. I can't get the bastards to the south because the Hajis to the north will cut me in half," Rick responded.

"You've a plan?"

"Well, sir, that roof."

Captain Kersey thought about it for a moment, and then said, "Okay. Listen up! First Platoon, I want you providing covering fire to the south and put some pressure on those RPG bastards! Second Platoon, I want suppressing covering fire on the northern targets and bring the LAW up here. Staff Sergeant Calderra, on my command, you get your ass to that staircase, and First and Second, unleash hell!"

Captain Kersey waited for everyone to get into position. Rick positioned himself in the middle of the road, directly in front of the staircase opening. The 249 SAWs and the M240s were in place. The captain looked left and then right. It was time. He yelled, "Aaaaaattack!"

Gunfire erupted so loudly it was deafening. It was echoing off the buildings. Even with the ringing in my ears, I still had to cover them. Rick ran across the road full-speed. So fast, in fact, that he slammed into the staircase, because he couldn't slow down in time. It knocked the wind out of him. After he got his wind back, he ran up the stairs while we kept up the suppressing fire until he reached the front roof door and entered through it. He opted for the front instead of the rear, which was further down the outside hallway.

There was a three-foot wall that went around the entire roof, which provided sublime cover. I watched him carefully as he crept towards the northern side of the roof to angle for a shot with the LAW. By this time, we had eased the firing so that we could draw out the Hajis Rick was targeting. Rick got into position and aimed.

I watched as he fired the LAW and a large boom followed shortly after, with a debris cloud covering the street. Rick looked over at us and grinned. He extended his right arm to give us the thumbs-up. We allowed a bit of joy to escape with our yells of success. Incidentally, however, we were so enraptured with Rick, we missed seeing the Haji that snuck out of the other entrance of the roof in the back. That's when it happened.

Rick's chest exploded with a crimson mist as three rounds from an AK-47 hit him from behind. They entered through his back and exited his breastplate. The sound was like a leather strap slapping a table three times. It was like someone had shined a camera flash right into my eyes; everything was tuned out and frozen in time. I shuddered in shock as my stomach went into a knot; my breath taken away like someone had punched me in the gut. I watched in horror as my best friend slumped forward, limply over the wall, and eventually slid down out of sight onto the roof floor. No, no, no, no, no! This was not happening!

I felt my body shudder as the surprise overtook me. There was no discipline, there was no composure, and everything I had been, everything I was, went out the window. Somehow the shock had a hold on me and kept me from the bubble of reality. Somehow I had generated a belief that what was happening wasn't as bad as it seemed. I still had hope, and it turned out that hope was a dangerous thing. There was hope that he was still alive and was just knocked down. I had to get to Rick; I would.

Captain Kersey's jaw dropped in disbelief. Immediately after, he looked at me with a shocked expression I have never seen the stoic commander exhibit. His feelings were evident. He saw my face and knew I was going to that rooftop. It wouldn't matter if he ordered me to stay, he knew I wasn't waiting.

For a brief second, Captain Kersey had seen the situation was beyond his control. That is dangerous for a battlefield commander, and usually happens when an event that he never thought could happen, happens. It's a tragedy I have seen eat away at officers with combat experience over the course of their lives.

I knew that a straight shot across to the staircase was not going to save the mission at hand. Instead, I needed to take out those bastards to the south, so I could get to the rooftop, bring up Third Platoon from the rear, and put pressure on the northern targets. The northern Hajis would probably light me up, but at this point, I did not care. I had faced death twice today already. Maybe a third time was a charm, and maybe now was my time, but I was not leaving him. By any means necessary, I was going to that roof to get my brother.

The captain was just about to order me to stay put, when he realized he knew better. He had known me for almost seven years now. I looked over at Captain Kersey, and he shook his head, as if to say, "No, don't do it." I could not listen. My brother, my blood, my family was up on that roof. I could not bear the thought of going back to New Brunswick and having to tell Mrs. Calderra that her son, whom I had vowed to protect, died under my watch.

I had to get up there. I called for covering fire, and the captain reluctantly obliged. The Hajis to the south needed to be debilitated in order for us to eradicate the remaining in the north. So, I took off. I ran through a field of fire that would have made General Smedley Butler proud. Bullets were whizzing past my head and all around my feet. One even got so close that I felt the wind as it passed by my ear fuzz, and it sounded like a mosquito.

As I ran toward the RPG nest, I grabbed a grenade from my load-bearing vest and unpinned it. As I got closer to the nest, with my momentum, I was able to toss the grenade into the window like a hook shot as I slid against the outer wall. The Hajis were taken aback by my ferociousness, and they did not know how to react to an aggressor attacking them point-blank, so they reacted in confusion.

I prepared myself as I watched the grenade do its job. Once it exploded, I observed an unfired RPG unit fly out of the window, with the arm of the victim still attached to it. I grabbed it amongst the heavy fire now coming from the north. Removing the attached hand, I aimed it towards the insurgents on the left side of the street. Bullets were now dancing around me, without inflicting so much as a scratch. From the ricochets, the dirt kept kicking up into my eyes. Fucking dust.

I aimed in the kneeling position and launched that RPG towards the left-hand-side Hajis. I winced as the thrust further hurt my aching back. There was a job to do, but the pain was beyond excruciating. I watched with satisfaction as the area exploded. With an all-clear from Captain Kersey, I proceeded to the staircase with my rifle at the ready. First and Second were still pinned down, because of the two Hajis now on the roof.

In retrospect, I often wondered how in the hell I was never hit in that sequence of events. Some used to say it was because I had guardian angels. After all, many events prior to this one suggested something was watching over me, not to be metaphysical or anything. But I did not care.

As I went up the stairs, I could hear the sounds of two AK-47s firing towards the east and south. Pausing for a second to assess the situation, I ran up to the third floor. As I was about to burst through the door, my gut feeling got the better of me. So I stopped myself and went to the back door. I could hear the Hajis firing; one on the south corner, one on the north. I knew the northern shooter was the assailant I was after.

With three short and deep breaths, I slowly opened the door. Concealment was my goal at this juncture. I spotted Rick slumped up against the corner of the wall in the southern section. He was not moving at all, and his eyes were closed. Both Hajis did not see me and were still too busy firing their weapons at those on the street. They did not know I was there.

This was a choice opportunity to impose retribution. So I aimed at the collarbone of the northern shooter, and then took stock of the southern shooter. My plan was to first shoot the northern Haji in the left shoulder and cause him to spin around so I could hit his right arm as well, taking out his ability to continue firing. Then I would unload on the southern Haji.

As I burst through the door, I did exactly as I planned. I hit northern Haji in both shoulders, then I turned to the southern Haji before he realized what was happening. I shot him five or six times in the chest before I turned my attention back to the northern Haji. Two more shots went into his legs, and now he was lying on the ground near Rick. The southern Haji was lying there, twitching. Just to make sure, I pulled out my M92 and shot him in the head. There was no compassion left, only vengeance.

I ran over to the northern Haji and picked him up. He was now face-to-face with me. I ripped off his facial cover and saw the evil before me. There was fear in his eyes as he looked back into mine. He was trying to pull a grenade to kill us both. Rage and fire engulfed me as I grabbed him by his pants and threw him over the ridge. His screams echoed all the way down as he hit the street below. I stood and watched a little pool of blood trickle out from his now-lifeless body; it all happened in a matter of seconds.

As I continued to lay a suppressing fire on the last of the Hajis directly on the street across from me, Third Platoon seized the opportunity and moved up the street. After about a good two minutes, they took out the enemy completely. We could all now advance up the road to the objective.

Once the area was secured, I turned to Rick. He was not moving. His eyes were partially open and he was not breathing. It looked like he pulled himself into the corner right after he got hit and they hit him a few more times. I opened his load-bearing vest and saw the extent of his injuries. That's when reality set in. That's when I knew he was really gone.

The pain from this realization was unbearable. So I shut down at this point. There is no way to describe this feeling other than absolute emptiness. It's a numbness that consumes your thoughts and awareness of your surroundings. I didn't know what to do for the first time in my life, because Rick and I had always done everything together. So I did what any Marine would have done. I sat behind him and held him until the corpsmen arrived.

An hour had passed while I was up there. Third, Second, and First were now able to move up the road and secure the area. Marines were now scattered around, regrouping from the earlier fight. The CO had wanted us to continue the push north, even though we'd secured our objective. However, Captain Kersey had given halting orders until I came down off the roof of the building. He figured I had just saved the lives of ninety-six men, it was the least he could do. Nevertheless, the Battalion Commander Lieutenant Colonel Quinn felt otherwise.

Lieutenant Colonel Quinn came storming into the area, screaming at Captain Kersey, demanding to know why we had not yet advanced. This happened in front of the troops, so Captain Kersey was none too thrilled. The captain respectfully requested a private session to speak with the CO alone, which Lieutenant Colonel Quinn grudgingly granted. They went into one of the cleared rooms.

This is what, I was told later, transpired.

"Okay, captain, you have a private audience. Why

have you not moved the company as I ordered? We are behind schedule, goddamnit!" demanded Lieutenant Colonel Quinn.

"Sir, with all due respect, my Marine is up on top of that building and we're not moving until he is ready," replied Captain Kersey.

"May I inquire as to why this guy deserves that, captain?"

"Sir, that man lost his best friend and I am giving him some grieving time before we cart away his body."

"Grieving time?!?! Grieving time?!?! Captain, you're holding this operation up because one fucking Marine was killed?!?! One Marine?!?! It happens, son! You're an officer, you know this! I don't want to hear any more excuses, get his ass down here now and get the company moving up the road!"

Calmly, Captain Kersey responded, "Sir, actually, I have been in combat, numerous times, in fact. You should have known that from reading my file while you were leading from your desk."

This enraged the CO. He took his Kevlar helmet off his head and threw it across the room. Oddly enough, he did so with such force it got stuck in the wall. The CO was visibly angry and trying to regain his composure, as any good leader would. So, he stepped up into the captain's face and said, "Captain, I believe you have your reasons for being insubordinate, but if you ever disrespect me again, I will have my foot so far up your ass that you will be able to taste whether I use Kiwi or Kangaroo shoe polish. You got me?!?!"

The captain backed off and responded, "Sir, with respect, we owe our lives to that man; every one of us. He saved at least ninety men today. Sadly enough, his childhood friend got killed in the process. Staff Sergeant Becze did what he did even with heavy injuries. He stopped a major ambush from succeeding, and we were able to repel the insurgents' reinforcements before they could get in place. That's the kind of bravery I have only read about. He deserves the time up there. I owe it to him. So do you, sir."

The CO looked at the captain, and his face relaxed. He acknowledged with a nod. Silently, he stepped back and looked around the room. After about thirty seconds, he calmly said, "Give him another five minutes and then move him out. We need to get moving, captain. I want you to take him and the body back to the rear base and have him patched up. Something like this is rare; it's special. I'll draft up the orders from my desk that I sit behind, for you both to accompany the body home. You boys have been fighting nonstop for two months and could use a break. If he did what you say, I don't want to lose this Marine to attrition, and Command is going to want to use this for PR, sickly enough."

The captain looked at the CO resentfully and said, "I'll get him down, sir."

"I want your full briefing on this when you get back to Camp Victory. There might be an important medal here."

As the captain was walking out of the room, he glanced over at the Kevlar helmet embedded in the wall. He looked back at the CO and said, "Sir, I think I taste Kiwi polish."

The CO allowed for a smirk, and the captain headed out towards the staircase, filled with disdain for the upper brass. He quickly worked his way to the staircase and ultimately to the roof. When he came through the front door, he saw me sitting back in the corner, holding Rick. Two Marines were the lookouts and the one corpsman was sitting down against the wall, smoking a cigarette.

The captain walked over. I could feel him staring at me, but I was still in my own world. My face had crusted blood all over it and my uniform was soaked in Rick's blood. My eyes were puffy on account of trying so hard not to let the tears fall. Occasionally, one tear would escape and go down the side of my face, which left a trail through the dried blood.

I can't explain what I was feeling at that moment other than pain. Really, no words can describe it. How many people watch their brother get killed before their eyes? I was zoned out and still in shock. Part of me still believed that Rick was playing a prank and would jump up laughing anytime now. But it never happened. His body was cold now, and his color had been fading.

The captain said, "Staff Sergeant Becze."

I did not move, nor did I acknowledge his presence.

"Staff Sergeant Becze!" he said again, this time with more volume.

Again, I did not move.

It wasn't that I was ignoring him, it was that I couldn't hear him. Some call it "tunnel vision," when it happens. I could only see Rick's lifeless body, nothing else. The shock affected me so greatly that I also had selective hearing.

The captain was about to get really angry when something shifted in him. How could it not, after he had known someone so well for seven years? He was a father figure, and it was as though he had just lost a son. He was having difficulty containing it, but as a combat officer, especially in Recon, he could not show any weakness. The captain took a deep breath, and then exhaled. He kneeled, lightly shook my boot, and said, "Bryan."

Somehow, that made me snap out of it. I looked over at the captain and I could see the empathy starting to build up in his eyes. The only thing I could muster to say back was, "Sir?"

"You have to get up now, Bryan," he said softly. "We're going to take him down to the Humvee and go back to Camp Victory with the rest of the wounded. We're going to take him home. I need you to pull it together and help me take Rick downstairs now. Can you do that?"

I looked at the captain for a moment and nodded. The corpsmen came over and helped me up. My lower back and shins were starting to really hurt, but the physical pain was held at bay by my anguish. Both Marines who were lookouts came over to help as soon as the area was officially cleared for movement. They wanted to put Rick on a stretcher, but I said no. I was going to carry my friend down the stairs myself.

Against the recommendations of the corpsmen, I carried Rick over my shoulder. Again, this was my family. He was going downstairs at my hand. The muscle tears would not allow me to do a cradle-carry, so I had to throw him over one shoulder. It was painful, but going down the stairs was easy. When we hit the ground floor, I came out of the staircase, and the Marines that were on guard in the area turned and watched silently as we loaded Rick onto the stretcher that was placed in the back of the Humvee.

I pulled myself up in the back and sat down on the flatbed floor. Four other Marines got in as well. They all had minor injuries, but severe enough to merit a Purple Heart. For everyone in that Humvee, our injuries, our pain, all seemed small in comparison. The captain jumped in the front passenger seat after giving a pass down to his relief officer. As soon as we were settled, he told the driver to head out.

It took a good twenty minutes to get to the base. For the first part of the ride, Captain Kersey kept assuring me over and over that I was a hero, but I felt that was bullshit. No matter what he said, I had failed. Out of the thirty thousand men of American and British forces, thirty-four lost their lives in the Battle of Baghdad. Thirty-four. Rick was one of them. When you think about it, that is one man for every thousand. That became a very bitter pill to swallow, and made things worse.

As our Humvee pulled into the gates of the rear base in Baghdad, I sat still on the flatbed floor, holding Rick. I was so zoned out that I barely noticed the F-18s flying low overhead towards the center of the city from the airport tarmac. Unbeknownst to me and prior to our heading into base, Lieutenant Colonel Quinn had radioed in to the rear command a brief report of that day's events. It would seem word had already spread throughout the base. Senior staff loves spreading morale-boosting word, and spared no time on this one.

The MPs perked up when they saw us approaching. They stood staring at first, and for a brief second, I thought they were going to hassle us with some sort of security protocol, but they didn't. We were waved through almost immediately. They came to attention and saluted. I normally didn't notice them saluting the captain, but this time they seemed crisper and had more meticulousness in their salute. It was as if they were being inspected by a general.

In through the gates we went, and on to the base

hospital. It was a makeshift hospital, basically a tent with cots, that hosted the wounded from the battles. Both the British and the American troops were there. There were Marines walking around the camp, who stopped and stared when they recognized the unit markings on the Hummer. I guess they never saw shot-up Hummer before. After what seemed like an eternity, we finally pulled up to the hospital tent.

For some reason, some genius decided to put the beer tent in front of the hospital. This beer tent was diagonally across from it. Nothing better than giving a wounded Marine 1,600 milligrams of Motrin and some beer. I could hear the Marines hooting, hollering, and generally having a good time, as most Marines do with their time off. There is not much else to do in the desert, especially on that day in April of 2003. The sounds of country music echoed throughout the area, thanks, partially, to the fact that the back half of the beer tent was opened up. That was, of course, until we began to unload the Hummer.

One by one, the four Marines who were in the back with me jumped down and grabbed a cloth stretcher from the hospital corpsman. The music from the beer tent had now been turned off, and silence encompassed the group. The partiers slowly came around to the front of the beer tent to watch, and there was barely audible chatter. I assumed it was because they had never seen a dead body, or, more so, that this was the first time they were seeing a fellow Marine killed in action.

We had always heard the old-timers talk about the loss of lives in previous wars, like WWII, Korea, and Vietnam, as if they were everyday occurrences, but this was different. Especially after we wiped Iraq out with little or no casualties in the Persian Gulf War. With all that technology, this was the new U.S. military. Losses were never to be high, if at all. Yet here we were.

As they slowly and carefully unloaded Rick, I felt sick to my stomach. I was lightheaded, and my chest was in a knot. Everything seemed slow-motion, particularly as I watched as they took his limp body into the hospital tent. It's a horrible thing, to watch something like that. In my entire fucked-up life, I have never endured a pain such as this. However, I did what I always did: sucked it up and buried it deep down.

As they disappeared into the blackness of the tent doorway, I hung my head. Blankness filled my mind. I was still spun up from the day's events. I was never trained for this; nobody is, no matter how tough they come across.

You know, it's funny the things you notice in horrible situations. I think you obtain a heightened awareness through tragedy. You begin to notice scents, colors, tastes, and so on. Things start to become more fluid.

SOUNDTRACK: Alice in Chains, "Rooster"

Amidst all that was currently going on, I looked at the horizon in the east as those two F-18s came screaming overhead towards the west. I watched them on a low fly-by on their way to bomb another target in Baghdad. As they passed, I followed them until they disappeared into the horizon, and I turned towards the city. It was then that I stopped and looked upon the most beautiful sunset I have ever seen.

Every array of the visible spectrum was displayed in the dusk sky. The colors became more vibrant than ever before. It was as though it went from regular television to HD. Up until that moment, it had been the most beautiful thing I had ever seen. I can't describe the feeling.

After taking a deep breath, I readjusted myself and slowly walked towards the mess tent. Adrenaline makes you very hungry, and chili mac was on the menu. I had seen it listed on the chalkboard outside the mess tent when we were coming onto the base, and my stomach was speaking up.

As I walked, it did not dawn on me that my cammies were still soaked in blood, and my legs were still bleeding from the pieces of shrapnel in my shins. Dried blood was still all over my face and hair. Every Marine on the way to the mess tent was stopping what they were doing and staring at me as I passed. I did not acknowledge them.

It was only about fifty yards, but it seemed like a mile. I heard the chattering of voices as I neared the tent. They all stopped as soon as I reached the entrance. I stood there as everyone stared at me in silence. That eerie silence would have bothered me normally, but not today. It must have been a good thirty seconds. Not knowing what to do, I looked around the tent. It was filled to capacity, and all the tables were occupied. To make matters worse, it looked like they were out of chili mac, and the chow hall was officially closed. Damn it, I really wanted some chili mac.

As I was about to turn around and leave, a group of Marines got up, cleared off their spot, and said, "You sit here, staff sergeant."

I looked at them, not understanding, but they were pretty insistent. Slowly, I limped over to their table as they asked me what I wanted to eat. I told them that I just wanted some chili mac and some grape-flavored drink. Remember, grape-flavored drink contains zero fruit juice, but all of a sudden, I had developed a thirst for it. The cooks quickly prepared my dish as I sat down, still out of it. Not once did it occur to me that everyone knew what happened earlier in the day. It was at this time that my lower back began to throb in pain. I was starting to come out of the shock.

The head cook, a sergeant, brought over my tray of food and put it in front of me. He told me to eat up and if I wanted seconds, it was no issue. Why was everyone being so damn nice?

Those who have been in the field can tell you, it is virtually impossible to get any food from the chow hall once it closes, let alone seconds after closing. I looked around and everyone was still staring at me with soft smiles. Still not aware, I looked at all of them as they waited for me to dig in. My eyes started to swell up with water. I put down my fork and put my face in my hands and just lost it. I couldn't hold it back anymore. Every Marine just stared, because they knew, they understood. No words needed to be spoken about it.

Captain Kersey came up behind me and put his hand on my shoulder to comfort me. "You saved a lot of lives today, staff sergeant, a lot of lives," he said as he gave my shoulder a gentle squeeze.

As I composed myself a little and looked up and around the area, I noticed everyone was still staring at me, though with approving looks upon their faces, as if to say, "Good job, Marine," without actually saying it. That was when I finally realized it.

The MPs at the gate had been saluting *me*.

chapter nine

REKINDLED

The captain and I were patched up within a few days. I had really pulled my lower back muscles something fierce, and was bedridden for three days. My shins were sutured, as the bones repaired themselves. It felt like permanent shin splints, and I was not allowed to stand. I had to lie on my back the entire time. I hated it, because all I did was think. I kept asking for more painkillers, so they would keep me asleep, but in the end, I persevered.

Two days after that we were cleared for travel, and they sent us back to Camp Lejeune in Jacksonville, North Carolina, so we could attend the funeral up in New Brunswick. Given the newness of the invasion, the logistics of getting a body back to the rear were difficult.

Our command was eating this up as a way to prove that morale was at an all-time high. They did not want to pass up on this PR gem. Captain Kersey mentioned that he had recommended me for an award for my actions in the field. He neglected to specify which award, but I rolled with it. Basically, that meant I was going to be doing a lot of meet-and-greets with top brass and politicians. I didn't give a shit, because the only thing a medal does is make your uniform look better and be a constant reminder of that day. It can't bring back your friends, or get rid of the nightmares.

I was to travel back to New Brunswick on special leave, be there when Rick's casket arrived at McGuire Air Force Base, escort it to the funeral, and deliver the folded flag to his parents. After that, I was to head down to Marine Corps Barracks, Washington, D.C., for temporary additional duty (TAD) until my unit got back to Pendleton so I could do PR for HQUSMC.

I was not thrilled about going to D.C., because that was where the entire USMC command element was located. Lots of high-ranking brass walking around, and they would pressure me to reenlist again. I was short and coming upon the "180 days and a wake-up" mark. This means I was about six months from my contract being up. I had about three months' terminal leave saved up, if I chose to take it. Chances were, I was going to re-up anyway. Stop-loss was in effect, for the time being, and would keep me from getting out until it was lifted, but I would see where this went.

From the moment we arrived in North Carolina, I was miserable. I don't know which was worse: Jacksonville or Iraq. In retrospect, I think Jacksonville. If you have never been to Jacksonville, North Carolina, don't go. It is a cesspool of the lowest common denominator of people.

U.S. Route 17 is the major highway there, and we used to call it NC-17, because of the filth you see in humans along it; it was not meant for the eye of someone younger than seventeen. The biggest thing that town had going for it was a Walmart. I remember hearing a car dealership ad: "Come on down to our car lot. We're only five football fields away from the Walmart."

Strip bars, tattoo parlors, barber shops, and Marine Corps surplus stores line the main roads everywhere. They have a mall with stores I have never heard of. I even had some admin POG (People Other than Grunts) gunnery sergeant give me shit about my civilian attire when I went to get a burger from Burger King. Are you kidding me? I so loathed that place.

Alas, they were sending me back home, to the place I tried so hard to escape. Once again, I was being pulled back in, to New Brunswick. I had to face Rick's family, particularly his mother. Maureen would be a separate issue altogether.

Prior to coming up, I had spoken to Mr. Calderra, and he told me there was a slim chance I might see my father at the funeral. Even the bastard drunk that my father was, every now and then he was sober and did something right. It was during that sobriety that the once-caring man came out. It was rare. Nonetheless, perhaps I could swing by and see him. That would at least give me closure on one immense issue in my life.

So, here I was now, right after leaving Tim's apartment, back in New Brunswick and standing in front of my dad's row house, my old shithole home once upon a time. Closure seemed like the only rational reason I could even entertain the idea of seeing my biological father. I had not spoken to him since 1987, when I was removed by DYFS, except for the times he would pass me on the street in his drunken stupors.

I always had to reroute wherever I was going as a child, to avoid him, even though the police told him to stay away from me. He blamed me for my mother's death and loved to terrorize me because of it. Furthermore, Lazlo had long felt I was a financial burden, because his wages were garnished every payday until I was eighteen, to go to the Calderras as child support. No remorse ever came from that man regarding my mother, ever. He never owned up that his drinking was the cause of everything. One night, before my mother died, he was kind enough to tell me I was the biggest mistake he ever made. Good times.

Once again, I digress. Looking at his house made me cringe, and my skin crawled with pins and needles. I was nervous. I had a quick flashback to when I was a kid still living there. That time he smacked my head into the counter, leaving me with a black eye for over a week. He told all the teachers and people who asked that I had tripped while walking up the stairs.

My blood began to boil. As I took a few deep breaths to calm down, I moved towards the front stairs. I walked up the stairs to the rusted screen door. I reached down to the handle and turned it. It creaked. The smell of body odor, whiskey, and bad breath came pouring out of the house. With contempt, I stepped inside.

I hated this place more than anything in the world, and the smell was just as it was in 1987. It brought back the horrid, vivid memories of my childhood. I walked into the living room where the television and the couch were located. There, in his favorite lounging chair, was Lazlo, snoring away with his head lolled back on the headrest.

I walked slowly around Lazlo towards the couch and sat down. I stared at him as he slept. Ten minutes went by before I kicked his foot to wake him up. Disoriented, Lazlo awoke, and almost had a heart attack when he saw me staring at him from the couch.

"Who the fuck are you and what're you doin' in my house?" Lazlo demanded.

"Take your time, old man, it'll come to you," I said and stood up, towering over him.

"Bryan?" Lazlo asked.

"That's right," I answered.

"You made it back? You made it back okay?" he asked.

I wanted to hate the man, but he seemed different. Maybe now that we shared an experience of war, we were brought together for once. Maybe, for the first time, he saw me as an equal in the suffering he endured in Vietnam. But he was different and not hostile.

"Sit down, sit down," he invited. "Back safe."

I slowly sat down and looked at him, as he blankly stared at me. Lazlo patted my shoulder from his chair and started talking. At first, it sounded like he was muttering. But the more he tried to stay awake, the louder he became, fumbling his words. A few minutes of this, and my disdain for the man began to fade. It shifted to pity, but most of all, forgiveness.

As I got up to leave, because I was losing my patience, he slurred one word that I could make out: "Proud."

I turned around to look at him and he was already passing out again. In his soon-to-be drunken slumber, he once more muttered, "I'm sorry . . . Sorry . . . Bryan."

Well, that caught me off guard. What was I going to do with all my angst? I was riding an emotional roller coaster until the bottle in his hand hit the floor. Blood trickled from his mouth as he upchucked a little. I was quick to check for a pulse. I began to worry now.

There was no phone in his house, so I grabbed my gear and ran down to the bodega as fast as I could. From there, I used the public phone to call 911. In all my hate, all my disdain, I could not let the man perish. It may seem odd, but I felt Rick would have never approved of me leaving him there like that, in that condition.

I watched from afar as the paramedics and the police arrived. A crowd of spectators began to grow, so I watched from that crowd. Lazlo was carried out on a stretcher, now unconscious. By this time, I was feeling much relief, and the knot in my chest began to loosen up. I could breathe again.

Later that night, I found out that Lazlo was unconscious and his bleeding ulcer had reached its limit. Apparently, he had severe cirrhosis of the liver, too. From what I heard through the grapevine, he was never to regain consciousness again and died about two weeks later. A part of me believes that Rick was there to make sure forgiveness was given, for my sake, before he passed.

As far as I was concerned, this chapter was now officially closed. I had been so angry I had no idea what to do with all that rage. Yet I felt a sense of relief that in the end, I caught the last glimpse of the man he once was. In some profound way, I was actually glad to have seen him. It was almost like seeing Darth Vader becoming Anakin one last time.

But yet again, I digress.

As fucked up as it seemed, it was time to relax a little and head down to Shenanigans for a few suds. I finally allowed myself to smile, be carefree for the first time in a very long time. It felt like I was back on my surfboard in California, catching that perfect wave. It was solitude at its best, a feeling of complete contentment. That was me at this moment, relaxed and fully deserving to feel so. A lot of buildup had been released that afternoon.

I continued in my happy effervescence until I noticed a familiar face on the porch steps I was about to pass. I could not place the face as of yet, and she, too, was looking at me as though trying to figure me out. Hopefully, I would not have to indulge in small talk. I was not feeling sociable, and I hated gossiping with the neighborhood jabber-jaws. She continued to squint, as if that would refresh her memory. As I passed her, I nodded, and then it hit me: Samantha, Maureen's best friend.

"Bryan?" she asked as I walked past. "Bryan?"

I winced, because I knew I was right. Luckily, she saw me do that. Pleasantries, it was all about the pleasantries. Samantha had, in the past, tried for many years to hook up with me, but I always rejected her—politely, of course. She was a sweet yet aggressive girl, now a woman, and not my type. Besides, she was Maureen's best friend and that meant hands off, even before Maureen and I got together. Still, that never seemed to slow down her determination to get her hands on me.

She was a very good-looking woman, by anyone's standard. She stayed in excellent shape: cheerleading, gymnastics, working out at the gym. Most of my friends would drool over her. They, including Rick, never understood why I wouldn't indulge her. It seems everyone has that one person in the course of their life who wants them, but reciprocation is just not possible. Nature is a cruel animal that way. But she was determined as ever, more so now that I was back in town and not with Maureen.

I turned to her and said, "Sammy? Sammy, how the hell are ya?"

She lit up like a lightbulb and her cheeks instantly turned rosy-red. She ran over and gave me a huge hug, rubbing her hands up and down my back, even squeezing my arms. Samantha acted like I was returning after being on the WWII battlefield, like that photo of the sailor and the nurse in Times Square at the end of WWII.

I was aware of this, as I hesitantly returned her hug. We stood there for what seemed like an eternity, before I broke free of her ever-tightening clutch. One more minute, and I was sure she would have raped me right there on the sidewalk. Given the circumstances, that may have not been a bad thing.

Samantha and I started exchanging pleasantries. It was time for me to hear all about the people that I had already heard about. Still, I participated. She was flirtatiously upset that I had not stopped by to say hello when I had arrived the day before. Even now, she was offering me a chance to come up and "have a glass of wine."

Even I, who is really not the most observant with women's signals, caught these. I even chuckled, but I was flattered. Samantha asked why I laughed, and I simply responded, "Tenacious." She, of course, smirked and told me her door was always open and it did not swing both ways. Of course it was, but I was trying to avoid the topic that was really on Samantha's mind.

"Have you seen Maureen yet?" she inevitably asked.

Again, I winced, as I was not ready to touch that subject. It was going to happen. I would see Maureen at some point in the coming days. However, I was not sure she would want to even talk to me at this point.

Briefly, I explained the letter situation. Knowing that she would run and tell Maureen everything, I strategically allowed her a little information, to bait the hook. Samantha reassured me that Maureen was not upset and that I should just go see her. Regardless, I wanted to plant that seed, because that was how I truly felt. Believe it or not, this maneuver tended to mitigate any discontent towards me when I had used it in the past.

After a good hour of talking and Samantha's attempts at molesting me, I was off to Shenanigans. Samantha forced a kiss on my lips to say goodbye, and reminded me that the offer still stood. I chuckled again, and was off to the bar. I had to admit, it was tempting, but not now. Maybe as a backup. I know, I am bad.

Samantha waited till I was out of sight before she ran to Maureen. It took her a good five minutes to get there in full sprint. Maureen told me all about it later.

Samantha walked in on Maureen and a guy sitting on the couch talking. Maureen was surprised, and made apologies to her guest for Samantha's rude intrusion. Maureen became very upset with Samantha, because this was a first date of sorts, and it was going very well. However, Samantha told Maureen to shut up, looked directly into her eyes, and said only, "Just saw Bryan."

Maureen's jaw dropped, as did her glass, and she stepped back in disbelief. Her heart started pounding through her chest. Maureen went into the other room for a moment to collect her thoughts, totally forgetting about the gentleman on the couch.

The guy began to put the situation together and knew this was not going to go any further. This was only a first date, and with the impending funeral, he did not want to cause Maureen any more drama. After a few minutes, the man graciously said goodbye and left.

Initially, I thought her father would have told her I was coming to town. He had not. Perhaps he did not want to be involved in that aspect. I couldn't blame him. After all, his son was just killed. Regardless, Maureen was still in her room, suffering from an anxiety attack.

Samantha tried to calm Maureen down, as she sat her on the bed. Just as I anticipated, Samantha began to relay all the information she gathered from her conversation with me. The usual was discussed: looks, attitude, attire, and so on. Samantha said I looked great, all things considered. She did point out that I looked worn in the face though, more so than most people my age. She could tell I had seen a lot and it was wearing on me. Maureen knew that if that was the case, I was still suppressing my anguish and negative feelings.

Maureen believed in her heart that I would return one day, but it had become more of a fairy tale to her these days. Eight years had now passed since she last saw me. As far as she was concerned, I was like a favorite dream: always remembered, but never real. She had handled the news about her brother relatively well, because she felt she had to be the strong one in the family now. Yet she was not expecting the extra weight of my being there.

The stress build-up made Maureen break down and cry. Rick's death finally caught up with her. Great. I was the tipping point. Samantha just sat there and hugged her. Eight years, five without a word, and I still affected her so. They say that you get one person, a soulmate, in your life, and I often questioned it, but she did not.

She started to compose herself. Enough already, she thought. She had to see me. Maureen got up from the bed and Samantha put together an outfit for her. It had to be sexy yet demure; she did not want to look too obvious. The outfit was a denim mini-skirt, a baby-blue tank-top, a denim jacket, and Burberry flipflops. She glanced over at Samantha for approval after checking herself out in the full-length mirror. Samantha nodded. It seemed my strategy had worked.

Maureen was ready, but it was too soon. She wanted to give me some time to unwind and be relaxed when I saw her, if that was even possible. I would have been jovial regardless, but she did not know that. Maureen drank almost a whole bottle of wine with Samantha before she was ready to go. She gave Samantha a hug, and her friend did not hide the fact that she was jealous.

Maureen stepped out the front door. It was time to claim *her* closure.

chapter ten

THE BAR

I was finally at my destination. However, this was not the Shenanigans of old. There was a huge line outside, and a velvet rope keeping people in place. It appeared the owners wanted to make this a trendy lounge. Nick was still working the door, with another bouncer. He sat upon his stool, guarding the velvet rope, rejecting those who did not fit the profile to be in Shenanigans; it had a strict dress code now.

I stood in front of Nick, who seemed surprised to see me back from overseas. I looked to his left to see how long the line was. It extended around the corner. This was not what I had been hoping for, and it started to cramp my evening plans. There was never a problem getting in when Rick was around. Nick was normally a dick, and would make me wait in line just because. I exhaled and began walking towards the end of the line.

"Where you goin'?" asked Nick.

I turned around and said, "To wait in line, dude."

Nick stepped off his stool, unclipped the velvet rope, waved at me to come in, and said, "Real men don't have to wait in line. You got me, hellhound?"

A small smile escaped me as I realized that Nick, for the first time, acknowledged me as a man. I walked past all the poor souls who were envious and resigned to waiting an hour, sometimes two, to get into the place. As I walked past Nick, he nodded and said, "No charge. Welcome back . . . *Semper fi*, brother."

SOUNDTRACK: Darube, "Sandstorm"

I stopped in front of Nick briefly, and he patted me on the shoulder before I walked inside. Talk about a change. The place looked completely different now. It was a contemporary lounge rather than the local watering hole. House music was now the genre of choice. Darude's "Sandstorm" was playing, and I could not help but think how much I hated this song. However, the mindless patrons loved it, as they crowded the dance floor. It was mostly white yuppies on the floor, and they could not dance, but nonetheless, it was thoroughly amusing to watch them try.

I have to admit, the atmosphere was good, and I did have a good vibe going. That meant the night was going to go well; it always did when that happened. I continued to weave my way in and out of people dancing, only to be groped a few times by some rowdy women from a bachelorette party. A typical wacky night, but I was on another mission tonight, because I knew in my gut that I would see Maureen sooner rather than later. I swept the area a few more times before spotting the guys at one of the booths.

They waved me over, and I said my hellos as I walked up to the table. After settling in, I began my surveillance of the club. It really had changed a lot. Things always do, that's always been a constant.

In the midst of the smiles and all the fun, I began to reminisce about the old days here. This used to be our place, the place we could come to chill out and relax with friends and not worry about the world. This place was where all the fellas and the locals would gather during the World Series, Stanley Cup, NBA Finals, and Super Bowl. It had been our watering hole. Now, it was everything cliché of the modern nightclub.

Beano and Tim began to tell their stories of Rick. I listened to their recollections in silence, surprisingly. Tim and Beano noticed it, too, and were trying to get me to open up about it, but they did not want to push me too hard. They saw that I was in a good mood, for once, and did not want to wreck it by dealing with the upcoming events. However, tenacity prevailed. Tim and Beano pressured me enough that I gave in.

I sat there for a minute or two. I began to zone out. The sound of the music, the people, and white noises began to drown out as I went into deep thought.

Flashbacks of Iraq entered my mind. It seemed no matter how hard I tried, something, somewhere would always trigger it. Sometimes, like now, it would just happen: the memories of fighting in impossible battles and impossible situations. Military specialists recently have been saying that it was because I have PTSD that it's been uncontrollable and unpreventable.

"Waking blackouts," I would call them. It was sort of like daydreaming, and it could be set off by something as trivial as the sound of champagne being uncorked or a balloon popping. Make no mistake, it was not controllable, and I hated that it happened. I hated that it had this much control over me. As I realized it was happening again, I winced, and the guys noticed.

Beano and Tim sat and stared at me for the duration, careful not to disturb me. They felt sorrow for me, because they knew what had happened in Iraq from reports on the news and online. They knew it forever changed me. I shook my head as Tim tried to snap me back to reality by waving his hand in front of my face.

SOUNDTRACK: The Moon, "Blow the Speakers (The Mighty Ghost Mix)"

A few minutes had passed, and the song changed. If you have never heard "Blow the Speakers (The Mighty Ghost Mix)" before, I recommend you hear it in a large club like Exit, Pascha, or something that large. While I was kind of getting into the song, I just couldn't let loose. They realized that jovial kid they knew in high school was long gone. The harsh realities of the real world had done their job well, and I felt like an empty shell, devoid of caring or ability to get attached. A few more minutes passed as I sat there, feeling more out of place and disoriented than ever. I started to spiral downwards. I looked at the patrons having a good time, and they disgusted me.

I began to grip my beer bottle tightly, and Tim and Beano noticed that my knuckles were turning white from the squeezing. I had developed much disdain for the people back in the States who were always frolicking around without a care in the world. It began my first time back from an overseas conflict that the government claimed never happened. It came at a cost these people would never know nor appreciate. This was typical for Manhattanites and Bennies, especially when they came to a club to party.

Manhattanites, if you don't know what they are, were the emerging self-absorbed "hipsters." To these Manhattanites, there was never anything outside the island of Manhattan that mattered, or that they ever cared about. These people thought they owned the world, and I despised them and their phony accents when they would constantly sing their words. They frequently came through New Brunswick on their way down to the Shore. They were normally the people with the "COEXIST" stickers on their cars. What else is new, it was typical in this area. Bennies are the same. The etymology of the word "BENNY" comes from people that are from Bayonne, Elizabeth, Newark, and New York. They are loud and obnoxious and are identical to the trash that was represented on MTV's *Jersey Shore.*

Nobody cared, nor did they try to understand what really went on over there. It only mattered when the price of oil went up. Matter of fact, most of the people here made us veterans feel like it was Vietnam all over again. Ignorance is always bliss, and Americans would rather turn a blind eye and watch Snooki.

I finally snapped out of it and turned to look at Tim and Beano. They were obviously concerned. I looked at them for another minute, feeling hollow inside, while Tim and Beano tried to act like they were not uncomfortable. Both of them had heard about instances of returning veterans snapping. Knowing my reputation, what I had seen in the Middle East, and, ultimately, Rick's death, they both felt like they were walking on eggshells.

Hell, I was notorious. It was my reputation that made them concerned. That said, I looked at them and managed a fake smile. To put them at ease, I explained that combat had made me zone out at times, and not to worry.

Post-Traumatic Stress Disorder (PTSD) is the most overused term in the American English. It manifests itself in many forms and levels, some more severe than others. We are not violent by nature. After all, we put our lives on the line to protect yours. That should give you an idea of where our heart lies. I don't deny that there are those who snap, but most of us will not. If anything, we would rather kill ourselves than hurt other people. Sadly, it does happen. I have known plenty who took their own lives at the end of their uncontrollable downward spirals. It's tragic.

I changed the subject by recalling one of my favorite memories growing up. It was the day Rick got his license. I began to talk. "It's funny the things you remember, you know? Going back to '94, late in the afternoon, Rick woke me up from a nap because his parents got him a car for his seventeenth birthday. He wanted me to come down and check out the new ride. Now, I was thinking he had a hot Camaro or Firebird, you know, the typical Jersey Guido ride. I must have tripped a few times running down the stairs to get to the front porch because I was so excited, even though I was still disoriented from my nap, and when I opened the screen door, there it sat.

"Glistening was the water still dripping off of this man-made beast of steel from its recent car wash. It trickled down over the faux-wood paneling on its sides. Brownish-red armor covered the rest of this beastly 1989 Dodge Caravan. There Rick stood, with a huge shit-eating grin on his face. He couldn't have been prouder. He called it "the Beast," and the best part was, he went and put a huge stereo system in it. I think it had two 200-watt woofers or something."

Beano and Tim laughed. They knew the Beast all too well. It was one of the hallmarks of our teenage life. So, I continued my recall with some panache. "Amazed, I inspected it, as I do all vehicles that I ride. I was mesmerized by it, because it was magnificent yet subtle. However, I felt somewhat dismissive of it until Rick made mention that cops would never pull over a minivan. Brilliant.

"So, off we went cruising the streets, blaring the 200-watts per speaker of Billy Joel on the system. The looks on people's faces were priceless. Nobody had seen a caravan with bumps before. I mean we were tearing it up. Shit, Rick even tried drag-racing a Dodge Viper. All in good fun, though. Of course, we got pulled over twice that day; once by New Brunswick PD and once by North Brunswick PD; both searched the car. Funny thing is, we had about an ounce of weed hidden in the 'Flux Capacitor' (secret compartment)."

They all laughed, and I took another sip of beer. Both Beano and Tim recalled their first time going for a ride in the Beast, and I continued, "We stopped and picked you two up, and, Beano, you had that crazy idea to do some drive-by egging of your ex-girlfriends' houses. Remember? That shit was funny. The best is when we told the bodega owner that we were making an omelet! HA!

"There we were, two a.m. in the morning and loaded with over four dozen eggs from the bodega. We strategically planned our route. The sounds of those eggs hitting the houses were one of the best symphonies I think we have ever created! It was fucking hilarious! Remember how we made it a point to hit all of our ex-girlfriends' houses? We hit one of their friends' house just to throw them off the scent so they wouldn't think it was us. Brilliant execution!"

They started laughing, hard. I needed this. For some reason, I confided: "Those things, the recall, where and when. Those memories come back at the weirdest times. It really is amazing. Rick and I were in Iraq getting hammered by enemy fire. There were wooden pallets stacked up next to a house we were fighting out of. I told Rick the rounds hitting the pallets sounded like the eggs hitting the sides of the houses we all egged. We both started laughing so loudly everyone thought we were fucking nuts."

Both Tim and Beano looked a little uneasy, but chuckled.

"You remember when we had De-Vern in the Beast?" Beano began, and we nodded. "I remember when all four of us with De-Vern did like that music video in the van when we were listening to A Tribe Called Quest's 'Scenario.'"

There were four in our crew, but De-Vern was strongly considered the fifth. He was often absent because he was always playing sports. He ended up going to UCLA on a full-ride for football and ended up becoming a lawyer out there. We all lost touch with him after 9/11.

To touch on what Beano was referring to, it was this one day we were driving around with nothing to do. The song came up on the mix tape, and we began to act it out as though we were in a music video, each with our own part.

Those were the thing back in the 1990s: music videos and mix tapes. Each of us in the crew had his own part. The vision of the caravan souped up with spinning rims and the guys jumping around on a basketball court filled our minds. Everyone in that caravan secretly thought of himself as the focus of the video.

Still, it was magic. I had thought of girls doing backflips and shit in a parking lot while we stood in front of the Beast, rapping. I began playing it back in my head and spit out my beer because I laughed so hard at the thought. I had almost forgotten that day, almost. It was buried by too much negativity.

It was about that time that Beano's kid brother, Rich, walked up. He gave me a big hug and cluelessly asked about the Marines and Iraq. Tim and Beano winced, as they knew I did not want to talk about it. Rich looked confused at the expression on my face, but then realized that he should have asked a different question.

It was explained to me that Rich was strongly considering joining the Marines. That made me think back to when I had been that excited about enlisting, when I had that glint in my eye. It was a long time ago, or so it seemed, especially after all that had happened. Rich was too gung-ho about it, as were most guys entering the DEP when they were waiting to go to Parris Island. I decided to talk to Rich, after all.

I began to break down my boot camp experiences to Rich, as he listened with enthusiasm, much to my chagrin. I talked about the yellow footprints, BWT, drill instructors, and so forth. I explained that there had been very few things in this world that surprised me about people, and not in a good way. However, boot camp taught you that people from all walks of life could come together and become brothers who would give you the shirt off their back anytime.

Case in point, I have never thought I would see a duffel bag weighing about seventy pounds get launched like a Joe Montana pass to Jerry Rice down the entire squad bay, but it happened, and I think that DI truly missed his calling. This pass did not make it to its intended receiver; rather, it hit one poor dumb shit, because he was not looking. Interestingly enough, I did find out that that DI was a combat engineer at his regular job. Those guys went out and found mines, so it should have not come as a surprise that he was all mental, too. Still, he should have been a quarterback. This made Rich's eyes get larger and larger.

Whatever, it was a learning experience and taught me a lot about myself, things I never knew. I told Rich that I wouldn't take it back for the world. It was definitely worth it. In the end, I was inducted into the largest brotherhood in the world.

Rich felt this was now the appropriate time to ask about Iraq. Tim and Beano both cringed in horror, as the question came out of Rich's mouth. I sat there in amazement. I hated these questions. People were always asking me, "How many people did you kill?" To which I would always reply, "Not enough." Typically, that would deter them from probing further.

I looked around the table and saw that everyone was definitely uncomfortable. I shook my head a few times and looked at Rich in annoyance. It would appear that Rich was still naïve in his thinking that war would be just like the experiences in boot camp. If I learned anything, it was that boot camp brought brothers together, and war took them away.

I slammed my bottle on the table, looked Rich dead in the eye, and said, "You wanna know about Iraq? Well, what the fuck do you think brought me here?"

Rich stood there, paralyzed. "I . . . I . . . I'm sorry, I . . . I didn't mean nuthin' by it."

Staring crazily at Rich, I realized my anger was starting to get the better of me. Solemnly, I patted Rich on the shoulder as an apology. Then I stood for a second and looked at everybody, figured it was time to go, and told them I was sorry. All three of them looked at each other and did not know what to do until, ultimately, Beano suggested they leave me be. "Let him get some air," he said.

The hard part was that I was rather disappointed with myself. My anger was always clouding my judgement lately. It was always a struggle, and it had always consumed me. Few things gave me solace. One of the easiest ways for me to calm my nerves was watching an episode of Bob Ross's *Joy of Painting*. Unfortunately for me, that was not available at the moment.

After wading my way through the dance floor crowd, I made it to the door and took a deep breath. Nick looked at me and asked if I was okay. He knew, but I nodded and started to walk down the stairs. I noticed a woman walking towards the club and I immediately saw who it was just from the walk.

Maureen looked up. Completely surprised, she stopped in her tracks, because she was not expecting me to be outside. Jesus Christ, she looked great. My heart sank, and I actually had butterflies in my stomach. I was twenty-six years old, and my heart still dropped. She looked even more amazing than the last time I saw her. Frozen, there I stood, not knowing what to do or say, so I let out a nervous, "Hi."

I must have played this scenario out in my head a bunch of times only to have it blow up in my face like I was a horny teenager getting his first kiss. Maureen was about to give me the "what the fuck" face, but instead she smiled. She pulled her hair out of her face, the way she used to do back in the high school days. Not fair.

This exposed that smile I had thought of so often in my times of duress. When I saw that, I exhaled and relaxed back into my comfort zone. We were now facing each other in awkward silence.

She gently and nervously said, "So, were you ever going to come and see me?"

After a few seconds of quietness, I took a deep breath and said, "I was . . . I just needed some time before I did. I . . ."

She cut me off, motioned with her arm, and said, "Well, I was coming to see you now, but it appears you are leaving. Did you want to get a drink?"

"I don't want to go back in there. It's not my cup of tea, this place now. Clearly, you saw Samantha."

"Of course I did, but you already knew that. Luckily, I have wine at my place. Walk me home?"

"I don't know."

Maureen almost lost her cool and said, "Oh no, you don't. You are not getting out of this. You owe me that."

I looked at her for a moment. A warmth filled my entire body.

I took another deep breath, softly smiled, and finally said, "Absolutely."

YOU STOPPED WRITING

SOUNDTRACK: Chris Isaak, "Wicked Games"

Maureen and I walked in silence for a few minutes along the sidewalk. We were both nervous. After all, it had been eight years since we had last seen each other. How does one even start this conversation?

She would frequently glance over at me and smile awkwardly, but every time the moment came to speak, we both clammed up. It was like we were on a first date, for the love of God. Inelegantly, I broke the silence by asking how her family was doing, to which I already knew the answer. Maureen responded, annoyed, that I would know if I had stopped by. Okay, a little bit of a burn on that one. Still the same old Maureen, still feisty.

Even though I had tried to avoid her, it was very refreshing to be near her. I felt relaxed, I felt myself again. Women like her are rare around Marine Corps bases. If you have ever been to or near a Marine Corps base, you know what I am talking about. There is a plethora of the sleaziest of the sleazy women, and they are no class acts. They aren't even kindergarten acts.

At Camp Pendleton, we used to call them "West-

PAC widows." These were the women who would take off their wedding rings as soon as their husbands deployed, and then go out for a night on the town. They knew Marines got a guaranteed paycheck twice a month, on the 1st and the 15th. Hell, they knew military benefits better than we did. They were known for getting themselves pregnant by drunken Marines to capitalize on this, yet Marines would still marry them, because it was "the right thing to do."

Rick and I were always dumbfounded by this, but it was true. They were also aware that a Marine could get in serious trouble with his command if he reneged on this commitment. However, the West-PAC widows could do whatever they wanted, without any regard, because the UCMJ did not apply to them.

The worst Rick and I had seen it was when we came back from overseas and one of the Marines was looking for his wife. She never came to the unit headquarters to pick him up. Little did we know that she ran off with some random guy she had met a month or so earlier. She was kind enough to clean out the bank account and the apartment before she left. But the final insult was that she left the television on a milk crate with divorce papers on top of it.

I personally despised a lot of military wives, but there are a lot of good ones. I adore those that stick by their Marine through deployments and terms of service, because it is by far one of the toughest things in the world. All that sordid trash did not matter now, since I was with Maureen. I had been gone for so long I had forgotten that most women in the world were not like them at all.

The moment finally came when we stopped walking. We now stood in front of Maureen's apartment building, much like that night we first kissed, when I was in high school. She still lived in the same apartment, because it was rent-controlled, even though the area had become extremely expensive under the mayor's new program called "New Brunswick Renaissance."

The program took down the derelict areas and redeveloped them. Her apartment building underwent its own renaissance, and was now choice real estate for yuppies and hipsters. From what I'd seen thus far, the mayor had been successful, for a lot of the run-down areas I grew up around were gone.

An eerie silence came over both of us, as we knew what would happen next, but neither of us could vocalize it. I even joked that this was déjà vu. Maureen snickered and realized that I would never muck up the courage to ask to come up, so she invited me in. Again, I looked around nervously, because I had planned to see her but not this soon. I was a slave to planning, and she was throwing me off. So I obliged.

Maureen's apartment was redolent of the past. The smell was the most distinctive, as it always was for me. Most memories I had of my past were based on a song or a scent. Baseball is the best example of this for me, because it was a constant love. One only smells a baseball used in a game to understand this correlation.

While overseas, I had carried around a baseball I had received from Wade Boggs at a Yankees–Red Sox game at Yankee Stadium in 1994. I tell you this, since there is always a scent on the ball. It was the smell of spring, the crack of the bat, the dust cloud from sliding into base, and a vibration from the roar of the crowd as we cheered the opportune instances. On a clear spring day, the air almost smells as fresh as a dryer sheet in the laundry. The leather pores in the baseball had always absorbed the aromas through play. This ball had been my happy place. When asked why, I simply replied, "A reminder of the real world." It was my talisman.

I felt the same way about being back in Maureen's apartment. I remembered the sanctity of her abode, which was always humble. It took me back to my days of innocence, if you can call it that. The unchanged ambience of her home was the last chance to realize I was not a monster, after all, but a servant to a cause. For a moment, I felt human again.

I leaned in the doorway of Maureen's home, just as I had done in high school. Looking in a sweeping motion, I surveyed the apartment, not because I was wallowing in the memories, but because I was looking for strategic places to mount a defense in the event that we were attacked by insurgents or terrorists. Sadly, this is a habit I have a hard time breaking to this day.

Maureen was in the kitchen, preparing the drinks, when she stopped to quietly observe me. She watched me check the perimeter, and knew I was different. She saw how unsettled I was, but understood it was not from being there. I was jittery. She remembered where I was a few weeks ago. It almost broke her heart to see me this way.

Maureen continued watching for a few more minutes as I stood motionless, in deep thought. She knew I was no longer the same person, but felt hopeful that I might be jovial again someday. Maureen was a dreamer that way. Still, she watched me silently. I would not move from the doorway. I stared into space. I really zoned out, but how could I not, with so many things I had buried coming back to the surface?

She walked up and nudged me with the glass in her hand. I shuddered like a little kid just caught for shoplifting Garbage Pail Kids cards. She looked surprised. Still, I could not look her in the eye. There was the inclination to tell her everything, but I didn't want to lay that burden on anyone. Ever silent, Maureen knew I would never talk without her breaking the ice. She tried, but could not help herself. She said, "You stopped writing."

Wincing, I looked at her somberly. Maureen acknowledged she had hit a nerve. But then again, I thought she was entitled. Not once had I let her know where I had been for all this time.

She walked into her bedroom and brought out a shoebox. I was a little puzzled by this, but curious. Maureen brought the box over to me and took off the cover. In it was every letter I had ever written to her. Every single letter, in its original envelope. Speechless, I looked at her with confusion.

"Every letter, every piece of paper that held your handwriting, I kept. I kept it because it brought me closer to you. I waited so long to have you, only to lose you. I kept them because I wanted to keep your memory alive to me," Maureen said, as tears began to drop from her eyes and she slapped my face. "What happened to you?"

Flabbergasted, I rubbed my face and fell onto her couch. I looked at Maureen sullenly. She was on the verge of crying, and looked distraught, as if I had dumped her at the altar. The only difference was that I had returned, and she was now looking for answers. She could not bear it any longer.

With great hesitation, I looked into her eyes one last time before I began to speak. "I've seen the most beautiful things in the world. I've seen schools of dolphins ride alongside of a naval carrier. I've seen humpback whales jump out of the water like submarines doing rapid surface drills. I've seen a bald eagle land on fence post five feet from me, in Alaska. I saw the most beautiful sunsets at Parris Island. I have been to every ocean on the planet. I have even heard, from inside of a submarine, whales singing. I've been to every state in the country, aside from Montana, and the Dakotas. I once even went to the Butterfly Pavilion in Colorado, where all the butterflies landed on me, so I looked like I was wearing a butterfly camouflage. There were these monkeys in the Philippines that would shit in their hands and throw it at us. Damnedest thing."

I chuckled.

Maureen asked, "With so many beautiful things, then why . . ."

I cut her off. "Because of the human factor. Only humans have the propensity for evil. In all my travels, I never saw anything horrible that wasn't created by a human. Christ, look at 9/11."

"I see. I kind of understand. I have had to deal with Afghanistan vets and their issues with adjusting with coming home. War is a tragic thing," she said.

"No, that's not it at all. The problem that veterans often face when they get back is not a hard time adjusting back into society; rather, it is that we've been all over the world and we've seen what is outside of the bubble—beyond the neighborhood, beyond our home state, beyond the Internet. You could say that we are just more aware than your average person of what is in the world.

We know that tomorrow is another day—and more often than not, it's tragic. It's like a recurring bad dream. Because we've been where we've been, done what we've done, and we've seen what we've seen. It's hard to have hope. After a certain amount of time abroad, it becomes surreal and as if this place, home, never really existed.

We come back home and see people obsessing about the most trivial things, like fashion labels, famous people, what car they drive, gossip, this person and shit, and more shit that won't make a fucking difference in a day. This trivial shit, as it were, is hard to care about after dealing with the shit we've had to endure. This is what makes it harder for us to adapt, because now we feel that we are no longer making a difference. Deep down inside, we ask ourselves if it all was worth it."

Maureen sat there, shocked. Never, ever had she heard me talk like this before. Always the compassionate person, she asked, "Well, is it worth it?"

SOUNDTRACK: Boyz II Men, "On Bended Knee"

At that moment, she was the most beautiful thing I had ever seen. I replied, "It has to be. When Rick and I were in this ravaged town in Iraq a few days before he . . ."

I felt a bulge in my throat and paused for a moment. Then I continued, "Anyway, I couldn't tell you the name of the place, because honestly I don't know how to pronounce the damn name. It was decimated by Islamic insurgents. They had tortured some of the people as a warning to not cooperate with U.S. troops. I mean, the shit they did . . . They even put one kid's head on a stick to remind the village."

Maureen gasped in horror. She asked, "That's what makes it worth it???"

"No. There was this little girl with her mom that I noticed while we were patrolling through it. She must have been five or six. When I looked at her, she waved and giggled. I stopped in my tracks, and just stared at her. Her mother looked mortified. I had a whole Hershey's bar I was saving for later, but I pulled it out and motioned over to her. I don't know why I did it, I just did.

"She looked at her mother, and to my surprise, the mother nodded and let her come over to me to grab the bar. When the girl took it out of my hand, she giggled loudly and ran back to her mother. The mother looked at me and let a small, thankful smile break across her face, and then they were gone. They made a connection with me even though bad shit could have happened to them for it. I never saw them again. But, in that moment, I actually believed in what we were doing there.

"Life has been nothing but a struggle for me. But every now and then, things like that give me a little reward, not much, just a glimpse. A glimpse is what keeps me going."

There I sat and just stared out into space, while Maureen softly put her hand on my face and turned my head so that I was looking into her eyes. She had a look that I don't know how to put into words. As if she was dying inside, but at the same time elated.

Then she kissed me, straight on till morning.

chapter twelve

THE FUNERAL

SOUNDTRACK: Moby, "Porcelain"

I remember the day vividly. I stared at my reflection as I began to dress up in my dress blue uniform. As I stood there in front of the mirror, my consciousness faded in and out while I put on another piece of my uniform. It was almost in slow motion, step by step. First it was my trousers, then my jacket, belt, gloves, sword, and finally my white cover. I stood there for a good three minutes, staring at my reflection in the mirror.

We arrived at the tarmac at McGuire Air Force Base just as the C-130 that was carrying Rick's casket pulled up from the runway. We waited for the plane to come to a complete stop before we got out of the government van. Once the engines shut down, the funeral honor guard headed to the back of the plane for the offload, while the immediate family waited at the funeral home, because they were not allowed onto the military flight line.

The cargo door on the back of the plane began to lower just as the sun had fully risen over the horizon. As the cargo door touched the ground, its rays lit up the Old Glory that draped the casket. The sun was shining on it as though announcing the arrival of Valkyries who had come to carry Rick's soul to Valhalla. It truly was a holy sight to behold.

Again, I felt sucker-punched. You can prepare yourself for days, but when you see the actual thing in person, the reality stings the hell out of you. The thought of this being a bad joke just disappeared, and the grief set in. However, I could not allow a loss of composure. That was my own private Idaho.

I signaled the honor guard to both sides of the coffin: four Marines on each side, with me at the rear. When they were in position, I gave the order to lift the coffin up and out of the military transport coffin case. If you have never lifted one of these, I can confirm that they are very heavy. In a poised and military manner, I called a soft cadence so that the funeral detail moved in unison as we moved down the cargo-door ramp and onto the tarmac. The hundred feet to the hearse felt like a mile.

After we loaded Rick into the hearse, I dismissed the honor guard to the van, and got into the front seat of the hearse. I sat quietly the entire one-hour ride to Boylan Funeral Home on Easton Avenue in New Brunswick. I hated this long ride.

Everyone on the New Jersey Turnpike would just stare as they drove past. I don't know what I was expecting, perhaps a horn blow, a wave, fireworks, but that was not realistic. As soon as they saw me in the front seat, people knew what was happening. Someone explained to me later that it wasn't a lack of respect, but the shock of seeing a real casualty of war. After all, that had not really happened since Vietnam. So this generation was getting its first look. I understand that now, but not then.

After we got off at Exit 9 on the turnpike and on to Route 18N, after taking the off-ramp of 18N onto Albany Street, we turned right onto Easton Avenue. As we crossed Hamilton Street, I began to see the cars for the wake.

As we pulled into the funeral home, some people came outside to watch us. Rick had already been embalmed and prepped in his dress blues before they shipped him to Fort Dix, thanks to Boylan Funeral Home making the arrangements. All that was left to do was display him in an open casket.

People impatiently gathered around us as we set Rick on display. In retrospect, I was angry, because Rick wasn't a fucking showpiece. He deserved a quiet moment before he was used as an object of other people's guilt for not having been a better friend or relative. In truth, everyone there felt guilt, none more than me, but maybe I was projecting.

Once he was set into place for viewing, I stepped out. I could not be social, nor did I want to pretend to be. I just watched from afar as everyone paid their respects, the priest gave a benediction followed by a prayer, and so on. In truth, I was just waiting for everyone to leave so I could be alone with my friend one last time. After about three hours of the viewing, everyone dispersed and a comforting quiet fell upon the room.

I sat down in a chair in front of Rick's coffin and just stared at his lifeless body. It didn't even look like him anymore. For what seemed an eternity, I had not said a word or moved a muscle. One of the corporals from the honor guard brought in my bag from the van. I thanked him and he left quietly.

I unpacked my sleeping bag and laid it out on the floor next to Rick's coffin. I precariously placed my dress uniform onto the first row of chairs, ready to go for tomorrow morning. Dressed in a T-shirt and shorts, I began to rummage through my bag when I found *The Raven*, the book by Edgar Allan Poe I had bought as a going-away gift for Rick. I had almost forgotten I had it.

I placed it under Rick's hands, where they crossed. His hands were ice-cold and stiff. To say it felt odd is an understatement. I closed the coffin ever so gently. As I lay down in exhaustion, I simply said to Rick, "No farting, bro," and I dozed off.

As I slept, my snoring, I'm told, echoed throughout the hallway. I remember waking up abruptly, disoriented, thinking I had heard other people, but I did not see anyone around the softly lit room. Unbeknownst to me, Rick's mom and dad had come back to say one last goodbye to their son. Poppa Calderra made it a point to not disturb me, and Momma Calderra began to weep quietly once she saw me sleeping on the floor next to Rick. Still, I never knew until after the funeral.

Morning came quickly, faster than most. The funeral director woke me up. I sat up, yawned, took in my surroundings once more, hoping this had been a bad dream. Still, no such luck. With a sigh, I got up and cleaned up before the funeral honor guard arrived.

SOUNDTRACK: Live, "Lightning Crashes"

The honor guard once more escorted Rick's casket out to the hearse in front of the funeral home. This time, we were caught off-guard by some of the people waiting. I again dismissed the honor guard to the van as I stowed my sword and sat in the front seat of the hearse. The Calderra family were following in the limo directly behind the hearse.

As the hearse passed them in the parking lot just before we turned left onto Easton Avenue, I saw Maureen in the front seat of the limo begin to cry as her brother's flag-draped coffin passed by.

At this point, I began to get angry.

I was angry at everything: the world, people, everything. Be it known that my rage was not displaced; rather, it was a misunderstanding. You see, I watched as people on both sides of the street went about their lives as if nothing had happened. Down Courtland Street and then onto Louis Street. Nothing, not a flag, not even an acknowledgment.

I remember now hating these people, because they never knew what we went through, nor did they even care. They hadn't a solitary clue of the shit we endured because it needed to be done. Every day was just another in a long string of days traveled through time. I was now questioning whether being in service of their defense was worth it. Was it? Then, and just then, my rhetorical question was answered.

SOUNDTRACK: Live, "Lightning Crashes," mark 4:03

On the corner of the intersection, I saw a young kid, about five or six, waving a small American flag. As we turned right onto Somerset Street towards St. Peter's Cemetery, there they were. As I looked down Somerset, people had lined both sides of the street. People waving American flags, signs, cheering as the hearse passed, there was even a banner draped across the street, which said:

SSGT RICK CALDERRA USMC 1976–2003
WELCOME HOME, HERO!

I dropped my head and nodded in approval as I exhaled deeply. I was moved, and this far exceeded any expectations I ever had in my heart or my mind. By far, it was one of the most moving things I have ever seen. Believe me when I tell you, no matter how hard-ass we veterans come across, deep down we always appreciate someone who genuinely conveys their thanks for our service, no matter how small the effort may be.

It turns out that the mayor of New Brunswick had spoken to the local news earlier and told people they should come out and pay homage to this "hometown hero," as he put it. Politics aside, the mayor did right by me, and by us. Rick was being given the hero's welcome he deserved. With that, I allowed a smile to creep back on my face, and my faith in people to return. That was the best send-off a Marine could receive, and for those of you who came out, I am eternally grateful.

SOUNDTRACK: Boyz II Men, "It's So Hard to Say Goodbye to Yesterday"

The USMC funeral ceremony is a beautiful thing to witness. Steeped in tradition, it is the perfect send-off for the fallen. There are specific events that happen before the Marine takes his final resting place. The flag-draped casket arrives at the cemetery by hearse. An eight-man honor guard carries the casket to the grave site. A clergy person reads a committal service. The honor guard lifts and holds the American flag taut over the casket. The seven-person firing party fires three volleys. The bugler sounds "Taps." The honor guard ceremonially folds the American flag into the symbolic tri-cornered shape. A properly proportioned flag will fold thirteen times on the triangles, representing the thirteen original colonies. When folded, no red or white stripe is to be evident, leaving only the blue field with stars. The highest-ranking officer in attendance presents the folded flag to the family with a slow salute and a brief statement of gratitude, which says:

"On behalf of the president of the United States, the commandant of the Marine Corps, and a grateful nation, please accept this flag as a symbol of our appreciation for your loved one's service to country and corps."

When we pulled up to the burial site, there was a decent-size crowd gathered around. As is the custom, we waited by the hearse until the people were seated. I had the detail at parade rest, waiting for Captain Kersey to give the go-ahead. The rifle team was also at parade rest, next to Captain Kersey while he stood at attention by the headstone. The seven-man rifle team and bugle player marched into position perpendicularly to the captain and came to stand at parade rest. The bugle player situated himself away from the people, just enough to where he would be barely seen, but could be heard.

When all was quiet, Captain Kersey drew his Mameluke sword, which was the signal for me to proceed. The rifle team and bugle player snapped to attention. With that, I drew my NCO sword and ordered the men to attention. At that moment, you could actually hear the sound of silence. I know, an oddity, but there it was, and not a thing disturbed it.

Slowly, in a silent cadence, with the detail stepping side-to-side, Rick's flag-draped coffin was pulled from the hearse. I stood once more at the rear of the detail as we slowly moved towards the gravesite in unison, as I called a soft cadence. Funeral honors are always done very slowly, so it took a few minutes to get to the casket-lowering device.

The sounds of weeping and sniffling surrounded us on all sides. It was almost as though the wind took the sound from one side and pelted us with it on the other, with an extra helping of anchovies. Slowly, in sync, our faces barren of emotion, the detail placed the casket down in front of everyone.

There we stood at attention until after the priest read some Bible passages. Then, the local base chaplain read the Marine's Prayer. Finally, the priest read a benediction, which concluded the religious portion. The whole ceremony took about twenty minutes. Now it was our turn.

I nodded, and the honor guard grabbed the flag, holding it taut over the coffin. Captain Kersey ordered the firing squad into the firing stance. The first shot rang out, and I jumped a little. Rick's mom bellowed. The second made my eyes tear up. The third was nothing but an echo of the first two, as the sound of silence filled the air again until "Taps" began to play.

After "Taps," Captain Kersey and I returned our swords to their scabbards. The folded flag was now about to be presented to the family, and both he and I needed our hands free. As the flag was being folded, I peered out of the corner of my eye at the Calderras. Momma Calderra was hysterical, but Maureen was poised. She was not crying; rather, she sat with a mournful look upon her face. She looked like she was trying to hold back, to be the strong one. Poppa Calderra was stoic, rubbing his wife's shoulders to comfort her.

The flag-folding was complete. It was presented to me as I slowly saluted it and gave the final inspection, as part of the ceremony. When I finished, I did an about-face so that Captain Kersey could present it. As

I stood there, I watched Captain Kersey step in front of me and slowly salute the flag.

It was at this point that I was to surrender the flag to him. However, I was not ready. He moved to receive it from me, but I did not let go. He looked at me, stunned. I was not looking at him. I was looking through him. I did not want to let go, because letting go meant letting Rick go forever.

Twice more he tugged at the flag and I did not let it go. This got the Calderras' attention, as they watched Captain Kersey trying to relieve me of it. Once again, he pulled hard to break my grasp, but I would not relent. Captain Kersey was trying his best to work with me there, but he was becoming a little frustrated.

Sharply, he whispered, "Staff sergeant! Staff sergeant!"

To his further frustration, I would not acknowledge him.

He let out a sigh, and whispered, "Bryan, I need you to let it go."

It was as though we were back at the top of that fucking building in Iraq all over again. I sniffled, as I finally released the flag into his custody. As I slowly saluted the flag, a tear escaped down the side of my face. I did not turn around as Captain Kersey presented the flag to Momma Calderra. Even the captain stumbled a little, giving the speech. Grief was staring to overcome him. Still, he held it together. The shrieks of heartache from Momma Calderra were stinging me. At this point, the ceremony concluded.

As the Calderra family tossed a handful of dirt upon the casket, the crowd dispersed for the reception. I wanted to reach out to Momma Calderra and give her my condolences, but she never once acknowledged me.

It was my assumption that she blamed me for her loss, and I did not want to agitate her further. I could not bear the thought of her hating me even more now, on the day of her only son's funeral.

Captain Kersey patted me on the back before heading back to the van. Maureen had broken off from her family to come over to check on me. When she did, I was still zoned out and heard not one word she was saying. It wasn't until she squeezed my arm that I came back to reality.

Somewhat discombobulated, I pulled away from her rather rudely. Without a word to Maureen, I walked over to Rick's coffin as it was slowly lowered into the ground. Once again, I saw the hurt on her face, but I had not meant to hurt her. Frustrated, Maureen let me be and walked back to her family.

No thoughts entered my mind as I looked down upon that coffin in that deep and dark hole in the ground. It seemed unwarming. However, I was finally ready to move on to the reception.

With that, I said, "Okay, buddy, I'll be back later."

And off I went.

Meanwhile, as I was told later, at the reception, Captain Kersey was making his rounds. He was very distressed about my situation with Momma Calderra, as he had overheard me mention it a few times in conversations. The moment seemed right for him to approach her, so he took it.

He formally introduced himself to the Calderras: "Ma'am. Sir. We met ever so briefly, but I was Staff Sergeant Calderra's company officer. I thought I would tell you about what transpired over there. It might give you some closure."

Poppa Calderra was not in the mood yet to speak of

his son in past tense. He said, "Captain, this is not relevant right n—"

Captain Kersey cut Poppa Calderra off with a little curtness. "Excuse me, sir, I think it is very relevant. That man, Bryan, is a hero because he saved the lives of an entire company. That same man who fought so furiously to get to your boy in his last moments. That man who had but one concern, and it wasn't for himself. That man, because of those actions, is going to be awarded the Congressional Medal of Honor."

With that mention of the CMH, everyone stopped and listened to the captain. He looked around the room, which had become silent, and then back to the Calderras.

"I just found out today, and I haven't told him yet. All I know is that I have known this man the better half of almost eight years, and I know he will never see it as an honor, only a reminder of tragedy. I need you to help him, because I cannot. He sees only the loss of his brother, not the saved lives of over ninety men whose families want to tell him otherwise. Here's what happened . . ."

Captain Kersey began to talk about the events of the day of Rick's death. People stood around in awe of what they were hearing, some even wowing. Maureen was in utter shock at what had transpired between her brother dying on top of that building and my quest to get to him. I really preferred the captain had never mentioned any of it to them, but it was too late, as by the time I came in, he had already finished. I could have gone the rest of my life without them ever knowing. Still, people were now staring at me with approving looks upon their faces. I thought it strange.

You see, I have never met a decorated veteran who brags about acts of valor. Rather they look at it as a tragedy, but civilians don't get this. It is a hard thing, to explain that valor normally comes from the deepest and darkest situations life creates. There are circles of hell that even Dante's *Inferno* could not conceive, which we have endured, and surely medals only bring back those memories every time we look at them. Furthermore, we normally do not feel worthy enough to wear them.

As I slowly walked into the reception area, I saw Momma Calderra sitting on a couch with family surrounding her on both sides, giving comfort as she wept. She was still clutching the flag tightly. I had prepared myself for this moment, rehearsed even, to ask for her forgiveness for the loss of her only son. I can tell you: I have never been so terrified in all my life. This very moment, and none other, was a first for me.

Fuck it, it had to be done.

As I walked across the room, the aging wooden floor squeaked softly with my every step, alerting everyone to my presence. That was not helping at all. My composure was already cracking as I stood now directly in front of her. As I was about to begin the speech I had rehearsed, she slowly lifted her head to look at me, with tears streaming down her face, and I froze. It felt like there was a frog trying to break through my throat, and her face broke my heart.

I could not remember a word, so I simply muttered, "I'm sorry. . . I'm sorry I didn't protect your son."

She just stared at me. Mortified and not knowing what else to say, I turned to leave when she grabbed my hand. Shocked, I looked at my hand and then at her.

She said, wiping away her tears, "We saw you last night. Sleeping there next to him." She paused, and I just stood frozen, looking at her, but fighting through her quiet sobs, she continued, "At least I still have one son left."

I fell to my knees, hugged her, and lost it. There was no composure to be had, no virility to maintain, just release. All the pain flowed out of my eyes along with the tears, as she hugged me back, and finally, I had some semblance of peace. People say that life is like a bowl of cherries, but all I'd ever had was the pits. This, this moment was the first time I ever got the fruit.

Finally, my soul could be at peace. For now.

chapter thirteen

ABSOLUTION

As hard as Rick's funeral was, it turned out to be a good day. Captain Kersey was kind enough to mention to me that I was being awarded the Congressional Medal of Honor (CMH). Seriously, it took him all of five seconds to tell me, in passing. Apparently, my actions so impressed both President Bush and Congress that they moved swiftly on the approval for it.

It was always my understanding of CMH that this was a big enough deal that merited a little more notice, just maybe. But he just came up to me and said, "Hey, you're being awarded the CMH in two weeks. You need to report to 8th & I down in D.C. in three days."

He then patted me on the shoulder, gave me the paper orders stating as much, and got in the van. That was it. That was my moment of glory. It wasn't like I was receiving this nation's highest military award or anything. Not for nothing, that is a pretty big fucking deal.

Don't misunderstand Captain Kersey's curtness though, he was immensely proud of me. It's just that he always needed to maintain discipline. He was never the emotional type. Typical lifer. For me, it felt unreal.

The sheer magnitude of it did not hit me yet, but it would when I would be shaking hands with President Bush.

Though, as most things in my life, it turned sour quickly. I sound like a pessimist, but I am actually a realist. I'd like to be optimistic about things all the time, but I know better. I hope for the best, expect the worst, because there is always another shitstorm on the horizon. Unfortunately, my next one was right around the corner, and I didn't even get a chance to breathe.

I spent the night at Maureen's place, and we decided it would be best for me to stay there for the remainder of my time in town. Off I went to get my things from Tim's place. I knew he'd understand. Hell, he had been practically pushing for it. Then, all of a sudden, a horrible feeling came over me.

Vinnie had mentioned that there was going to be a grace period to grieve for Rick, but I did not think he meant it was to end literally hours after Rick's burial. I was not sure what he had been planning, but I began to hurry. The closer I got, the sicker to my stomach I felt.

As the corner of Tim's street drew nearer, I saw the beams of red and blue flashing lights. His body was already coming out of the building on a stretcher—black body bag and all. Beano, visibly distressed, was talking on his cell phone until he noticed me walking towards him.

A despondent look came over Beano's face as he said to me, "He hung himself."

I replied, "What?!? We were just with him yesterday. No, no, no, no! Bullshit!"

"You haven't been here, Bryan. He's been a mess until you came back. Maybe . . . Maybe Rick's funeral pushed him over."

"But not his debt to Vinnie, right?"

Beano looked down. This was the moment Detective Lombardi of the New Brunswick PD seized the opportunity.

"I gather you're Bryan? I'm Detective Lombardi," he said.

"Great fucking detective work," I quipped. Given the circumstances, I couldn't help it.

"Ahhhh, Bryan, I am not the guy you wanna give attitude to right now. However, I'm in a rather frosty mood and wanting to give atonement. I'm going to give this another whirl. Do you know of any reason that he might want to end his life?"

"Look, he seemed fine. I haven't seen him in eight years, but he seemed fine while I have been here. Something on your mind, detective?"

"Well, his suicide note is what seems to puzzle me. What does it mean to you that he wrote 'PAID IN FULL'?"

Right then and there my face went from shock to anger. That was all the confirmation I needed. It was hard to conceal, and Lombardi noticed it, too. Detectives notice everything. Nevertheless, I played dumb. The detective went through the motions and gave me his card in the event I could think of anything.

By this time, Maureen had shown up. It turns out she was the one Beano was on the phone with. She, too, was frantic, but I was in no mood to comfort her. Vengeance was going to be mine, believe me. She looked at me, and I gave her a stare that made her realize I had stepped into the red zone. Still, Maureen being Maureen, she had to try.

There are no words to describe my thought process at this moment, because I was devoid of thought. Animal instinct overcame me, and rationale had gone out the window. Maureen was trying her best to calm me as I stomped down the sidewalk towards where Vinnie and his crew normally hung out. This rage was not to be quelled. Even I felt scared of my own uncontrollable, rage-fueled quasi-consciousness.

Maureen gave up after about a hundred feet, hopping up and down in a panic, compelled to stop me. In retrospect, this was one moment I wish I really could erase from her memory. The helplessness she must have felt was probably similar to what I felt when I saw Rick's chest explode. Luckily, Beano was not far behind, and he was able to hold her back enough to where they could follow me at a safe distance. I really am sorry for the pain I have caused her.

By this time, I had already reached the building where Vinnie hung out with his crew. They had a basement dwelling, where they gathered to play cards and such. It was best described as a ramshackle rec room, like a back-alley garage. I walked through the front door at street level and took the stairs down. I reached the door at the bottom floor and with one swift kick knocked the door off its hinges and into the room.

Now, I would love to toot my strength as superhuman, but the door was a piece of shit, two layers of veneer glued together. Besides, I had done enough breeching to know exactly where to kick a door to dislodge it. However, Vinnie's crew didn't know this, and it scared the shit out of them something fierce while they were playing poker at the table.

They got up quickly to try to make sense of what happened, as I stood there in the doorway, breathing heavy with rage. I gave it a second as I looked around the room to locate Vinnie, and he was expecting me. As he slowly stood up, smirking, the little bastard asked, "Where's Tim? Still hanging out?"

SOUNDTRACK: Rage Against the Machine, "War Within a Breath"

Without hesitation, I lurched towards him as he tried to say something else that was bound to enrage me further.

I would like to tell you I said something cool, or did something theatrical, like backflips with a Chuck Norris roundhouse and nunchucks, but this is not the movies. The reality was all too real. I had a preconceived notion of how this was going to play out, and that I had something cheesy but memorable to say. Alas, I have never been able to form sentences when I am angry, which is why I have been in so many fights.

It was not graceful, because I felt angrily cumbersome. Nonetheless, I was able to flawlessly land the hardest punch I have ever thrown on Vinnie's forehead, where it meets the bridge of the nose. The force was so great, he flew back onto the poker table and broke the corner section off, leaving a table leg exposed. Once again, his crew was taken aback by my actions and just stood there, bewildered.

Vinnie, still stunned, on his back, slowly picked himself up and dusted himself off. A bump started to form on his forehead. One of the crew decided to take a step towards me, and he yelled, "No! He's mine." Wiping the dust off his eyebrows, he continued, "Okay, let's do this!"

No words came from me, and I just stood there ready to go. So it began, the championship fight, and we squared off. Vinnie, always the aggressor, threw the first punch. It did not go according to his plan. I ducked as his fist flew overhead. My own fists began quickly pounding on his kidneys and ribs, with an uppercut to knock him back down. Let me be clear: I was not there to make a big production, nor a point. I was not there to eliminate, but punish and punish I did.

Part of me wanted to admire the guy for continuing to get up. It was almost like he was doing it to pay for what he did to Tim. One might even think he had some guilt. I'll never know, but I knocked him down again and again. Finally, I saw him starting to crumble. Still, not one of his crew stepped in to stop it. Now, he was breathing heavy, on all fours, a bloody mess.

SOUNDTRACK: The Smashing Pumpkins, "Bullet with Butterfly Wings," 3:05 mark

"Get up! Get up, motherfucker! I'm not done yet," I barked.

Vinnie looked up, picked himself up, and grinned while bloody saliva slowly trickled from his chin. He got into his fighting stance once more, and began to pull his fist back. Before he could even bring it forward, I was on him with a multitude of hit combos. Down he went a second time.

Vinnie was even more sluggish getting up this time. It was almost as if he was really drunk. With his arms limply swinging as he stood upright, you could see the damage to his face. His eyes were swollen, his lips split, and his nose bleeding. It was time to end this, and with one last uppercut to his jaw, I did.

Vinnie flew back limply once more, but this time he made an unfamiliar noise once he landed. Motionless, he lay on his back, and even I noticed it was odd. That was when everyone in the room panicked and ran out so I was the only one who remained.

In my rage, I had not been wary of my surroundings. Vinnie's head had come down on the exposed leg of the broken table. It had pierced the back of his skull, killing him instantly. I stood over him with my fists still clenched. It took a little time to register that he was dead. Thankfully, Beano came in behind me to bring me back to reality.

Beano shook me a few times to snap me out of it. When I finally came to, I asked when he arrived. He stressed the importance of me vacating the area as soon as possible. By area, he meant New Brunswick. He did not want me at the scene.

Quickly, we left and were unseen, to the best of my knowledge. Beano was able to get my seabag from Tim's place after the forensic people left. With Maureen in tow, Beano drove me to the New Brunswick train station on French Street. Maureen walked me up the stairs to the platform. This all happened in a matter of twenty minutes. To her credit, she was handling this very well. Then again, I have always had a lot going on around me and this was par for the course.

She looked at me and shook her head, then said, "Every time we take one step forward, something puts us two steps behind. We can never get a break."

"Maybe I'm damaged goods, kid," I said, exhausted.

"Nonsense," she replied. "Always in the wrong place."

As the Amtrak train to Washington, D.C., arrived, I gently cupped her face in my hand. She leaned into it and I kissed her. I looked at her once more and tried to say something, but nothing came out. My mouth started to move; no sound came from it. Maureen told me she knew what I was going to say, but just get on the train and call her once I got down there. I obliged.

It wasn't until I was on the train for an hour that I came to the realization that she was waiting for something, anything, to come out of my mouth. Again, it was not like the movies. No romantic ending with a knight on his white horse. It was painfully awkward, but given the previous twenty minutes, I have to say I was remarkably composed.

My hands were a little scuffed, but I was able to clean them in the crappy bathroom. I found a window seat. I rested my head against the glass and dozed off. In a little under three hours, I was at Union Station, Washington, D.C.

After waking up, I grabbed my stuff and looked around to see if I was being greeted by police. There were none. I paused in front of a payphone for a moment, with every intent of calling, but instead walked outside to the cab stand. About fifteen minutes later, I arrived at the sentry gate for USMC Barracks, Washington, D.C.

After a quick screening, I was allowed access. The MP was kind enough to admit me early and have my room set up ahead of time. When I got settled in, I called Maureen, only to let her know I got there okay. She told me there had been inquiries about Vinnie, but nothing leading to me, at that point. Reluctantly, I hung up with her so I could get some rest.

When I got back to my room, I sat there on the bed for a long time. I wish I could tell you just how long, but I honestly don't remember. I did not move, and the sound of silence was driving me mad. What a fucking week. When I come home, I come home.

I thought it would not be long before an MP would

be coming to arrest me at the behest of Detective Lombardi. Just the thought of being in Middlesex County jail was gut-wrenching. Yet it never came. As luck would have it, nobody back home would speak of the incident publicly, or to the police. Even Vinnie's crew was silent. I guess they had enough of him; time for new blood.

So I fell onto the pillow, exhausted, and fell asleep. I was too tired to take off my clothes, and they stank of adrenaline. Regardless, the next chapter of my life was to begin tomorrow. Imagine my surprise when I awoke from my slumber, thanks in part to the morning reveille bugle. 8th & I used a real bugle and it was loud.

To give you a bit of a background, 8th & I, or Marine Barracks, Washington, D.C., is aptly named for its location. Founded in 1801, it has been the home of the commandant of the Marine Corps since 1806. The Silent Drill Platoon, U.S. Marine Drum and Bugle Corps, and the U.S. Marine Band all call it home. This is where most major Marine Corps ceremonies take place.

As with such, there were no expenses spared at this place. Even my bunk was tip-top. I had a real blanket instead of that abysmal woolly-green thing they issue us, that feels like a Brillo pad, with "US" stamped on it in big letters. The chow was top-notch, especially the chili mac. I did feel out of place with all the brass walking around, not to mention seeing the commandant's house.

My luck, if I do have any, does manifest itself in an odd way. For example, the timing for my check-in was perfect. The awards ceremony was to be in a week, and then I was going back to Camp Pendleton. This made my hastened departure from New Brunswick all the less suspicious. Even for a detective, it would have been hard to question my wanting to get down here as quickly as possible after Rick's service to accept my medal. On the other hand, I really didn't give a shit about the medal.

I was supposed to report a week from now, but I knew they would take me early. I was their wet dream for PR and recruiting. Apparently, Lieutenant General Earl B. Hailston, General Michael William Hagee, and Major General James "Mad Dog" Mattis would all be in attendance. Maureen and Beano wanted to come down for the ceremony, but I did not want them there. Naturally, they did not understand why.

It was not to be rude or inconsiderate to them; they just would not understand. They saw the medal as an award, a recognition of a heroic act. I saw it as a reminder, a painful reminder. For me, that reminder I feared would always be thrust into my face, forcing me forever to seek an answer to the question "what if"?

So I did a lot of ceremonies and hobnobbing with the political groupies of Washington, D.C. I made it a point to be as crude and swear as often as I could, because I was not enjoying myself, by any means. Hitherto, it wasn't until President Bush put the CMH around my neck and shook my hand that I, all of a sudden, had an epiphany. My realization was that I could do nothing more in the Marine Corps. There was nowhere to go from here, nothing more to learn. I finally had it, but I kept it quiet.

After the White House ceremony, I was off to another ceremonial meet-and-greet. I would like to think I was upbeat about everything, but the last few days were killing me. I had already begun distancing myself from Maureen yet again, and from New Brunswick. At least the dust had settled from the Vinnie incident, and

Detective Lombardi did not seem interested in me as a suspect.

Needless to say, there was a lot on my mind, but this medal I now wore hung heavy on my shoulders. I must have looked sullen when I caught Major General Mattis heading my way. As I snapped to attention, he firmly shook my hand, congratulating me, but he noticed I was unenthused and asked what was wrong.

A few seconds passed before I replied, "I don't feel I earned this, sir. I don't think I deserve . . ."

Interrupting me, he put his hand on my shoulder, looked me dead in the eye, and said, "Son, it's never about you. It's about them." He pointed randomly around the room at other uniformed Marines. "Without them, you would have never done what you did that day. It's our brotherhood that makes us go above and beyond for each other. Don't you ever fucking forget that, Marine."

It then occurred to me that this was why he was a general. His admonition humbled me. I nodded in acknowledgment as he patted my shoulder before walking away to talk to more people who were above my pay grade. We need to hear shit like that from people like him. It's moments like these that make you understand why we revere General "Mad Dog" Mattis.

These PR functions continued in the days that followed. I was exposed to a lot of dignitaries, high-ranking generals from across the military, numerous politicians, NSA, CIA, DHS, and so on. For some, this was an ideal place to be. Me, however, I just wanted out of there. I felt like a new car being shown off to its owner's girlfriend so he could get a hand job—just as sticky, too. Besides, I was never one for bureaucrats, nor their utter ignorance of reality. Remember, you can't have "pro-gress" without "con-gress."

But I digress.

The top brass had been very inquisitive about my thoughts of staying on in the Marines for the duration. Admittedly, it was nice to be courted so heavily, but I felt this was nothing more than a façade to get me to do more PR. HQMC went as far as to meritoriously promote me to gunnery sergeant. Not bad for a guy who had been in less than ten years.

I had met with General Hagee and Lieutenant General Hailston more than once during this time, and they both tried like hell to sell me on the good life. Furthermore, they went as far as to tell me how cushy it would be for me from here on out. Unbeknownst to me, the CMH had come with some perks:

* A special Medal of Honor pension every month in addition to any military pensions or other benefits for which I may be eligible.

* Special entitlements to Space "A" air transportation (free military flights anywhere in the world).

* Admission to the U.S. military academies for qualified children of recipients, without nomination and quota requirements.

* Medal of Honor flag.

* Medal of Honor automobile license plates.

* Interment at Arlington National Cemetery.

Now you know. I never did, nor had I ever thought about any of that until Lieutenant General Hailston made mention of it. He was really pushing me to reenlist and come to 8th & I in Washington, D.C. In the end, as I stated before, I really didn't care. I just wanted my friend back.

I had my choice of any duty station and/or assignment I wanted. Hell, I could become a commissioned officer if I so desired it, but I would still have to attend Officer Candidate School. It was very enticing, and they made a good case. However, the generals needed to know as soon as possible, because my EAS, or end of active service, was fast approaching. There was a lot going through my mind. Too much to process all in such a short amount of time.

I had briefly touched base with Maureen, and she was back in New Brunswick, twiddling her thumbs yet again, waiting to hear what I would do next. Moreover, I had not talked to her much at all, so she was getting detailed updates from Beano. He told her it was probably because I had not wanted her influencing my decisions. Naturally, this hurt her feelings, but it was not meant to do so. I simply refused to be swayed by emotion.

I saw the generals the next day. The morning was windy but sunny. I was escorted by the commandant's adjutant into General Hagee's office. Lieutenant General Hailston was already seated in the chair adjacent to Hagee's desk. General Hagee ordered me at ease as he finished going through his desktop paperwork. He was not for a fan of computers, so killing trees was paramount.

Generals aren't ones for small talk, because General Hagee wasted no time by looking up at me and asking, "So, Gunnery Sergeant Becze, what's it going to be?"

The day had finally come to make a decision, and I made it.

chapter fourteen

DD-214

It's a harrowing thing, making the decision to quit something you love. You lived and breathed it day after day, year after year. It's not just a job, it's a lifestyle. You fought for the right to be it for three hellish months, and endured countless hardships to maintain the title. It's who you are, right down to your very soul. That very same soul that dies a little every time you bury a brother—and believe me, they are family. Burdensome it becomes, but this may give you a little perspective as to why I have decided to leave the Marine Corps. It wears you out, and I was exhausted.

My unit just got back from the invasion tour. Sergeant White kept looking at me as he drove us to our unit building. He was silent. I knew he wanted to say something, something worthwhile, but the words were never spoken. It was evident that he was not pleased I was leaving. After all, without Rick and me, Denzel would be by himself. On a side note, White was just promoted to staff sergeant after having been passed over once before. That pretty much cemented his career choice. Normally, if a Marine is passed over, it's very unlikely a promotion will ever happen, but he was the exception. You see that a lot: Marines who want to stay

Marines never getting promoted. But his recent achievement seemed overshadowed by his concern for me.

Finally, he spoke. "You sure you wanna do this, B? I mean, are you really sure, bro?"

I looked at him sullenly and said nothing. White nodded in acknowledgment without saying a word, and turned his attention back to driving. We were almost there, and I immersed myself in thought once again as we passed the air station on Vandegrift Boulevard in Camp Pendleton. We then made the left onto Basilone Road towards Camp Margarita. Finally, we made the left onto Stagecoach Road and into Camp Margarita.

As we pulled into the battalion parking lot, I noticed that it was virtually empty in front of the battalion headquarters. I thought that was unusual, considering it was 0757 in the morning. Sure, there were Marines walking around, but I thought it was odd that there were no cars in the parking lot. Even though I was trained to notice things out of the ordinary, I ignored it, because I was picking up my DD-214 today. White pulled into one of the parking spots marked "SNCO," a little away from the battalion HQ building.

As we got out of his pickup truck, Denzel let a smirk escape from the corner of his mouth, knowing that by the time we walked across the parking lot, "Morning Colors" would be sounding. One last time, for old times' sake, I guess.

As the speakers in the area played the bugle, we both came to attention and saluted the Old Glory as the Color Guard hoisted her into the air. That day, she seemed more vivid in color as she flapped in the wind. For me, this was the very last time in uniform.

Once the ritual was completed, we went into the

battalion headquarters and White walked with me over to the battalion CO's office. As we came near the office, White looked at me and gave me a friendly pat on the shoulder. The entire time, he said nothing, and now he left to attend to his duties.

The adjutant acknowledged my presence and informed Lieutenant Colonel Quinn I had arrived. As with most COs, it must be a customary thing to make people wait ten minutes before seeing them. It was as if by some chance I would just throw up my hands and say, "Well, fuck it, I'm staying in!"

Finally, the adjutant motioned for me to report to the CO. Up I stood and walked into the CO's office. As I came to attention in front of his desk, I noticed Captain Kersey seated in the corner. Lieutenant Colonel Quinn told me to take a seat.

"So," he began. "Today is the day, eh?"

"It would appear, sir."

"Lieutenant General Hailston, Captain Kersey, and I wanted see about persuading you otherwise. Now, before you respond, think about this, is there another job you really want to do? If you are having doubts, a meritorious promotion to gunnery sergeant and winning the Congressional Medal of Honor should indicate that you were born for this line of work. We need leadership like yours in here to benefit the young Marines coming up. Captain Kersey has even recommended you as an instructor. The secretary of the Navy has already agreed to sign off on it. What do you think, son?"

"Sir, with all due respect, my answer has to be no."

Lieutenant Colonel Quinn blinked his eyes in disbelief and then asked, "Think again, gunny. One more time, will you stay Marine?"

"Let me ask you this, sir, if all I do is fight, what is

my reward? Some stripes and medals? Buried friends and tattered injuries that are going to be plaguing me before my fortieth birthday?" I responded.

"You're a little out of line, don't you think?" Lieutenant Colonel Quinn asked.

"That's a pretty loaded question, don't you think, gunny?" Captain Kersey echoed.

"No, sir," I responded. "I think it's pretty straightforward. If you think it's a loaded question, it's clear to me that it will never be answered. Not here at least."

Lieutenant Colonel Quinn raised an eyebrow, but was otherwise stoic. He sat back in his chair and tapped the desk with his fingers.

"It's a harsh world out there, son . . ." he began to say.

"As opposed to here? The Middle East? The next Third World shithole I get sent to? Sir, if I don't take this leap, I never will. You want me to enrich the minds of the young, let me get them in college. Perhaps I can dare some of the little shits into signing up. You'd like that, wouldn't you, sir?"

Captain Kersey rolled his eyes and then looked at me with a rather annoyed look on his face.

Lieutenant Colonel Quinn reared up to give me an ass-chewing for the insubordinate comment, but held back. He looked at me and said, "I'm really not going to miss your fuckin' mouth, gunny."

"Aye-aye, sir," I responded with a smirk. This was the only time I could ever get away with this kind of insubordination, so I enjoyed it.

He was visibly annoyed, but held his disdain in check. I thought that was going to be my last impression on Lieutenant Colonel Quinn, but he continued, "But a finer Marine, in my experience, there never has been."

I was so shocked at what I just heard from the grumpy bastard that I actually replayed it in my head for about thirty seconds. Even Captain Kersey showed a little bit of shock, but not much.

Lieutenant Colonel Quinn stood up from his desk, extended his hand to me, and said, "Well, then that's it."

When I went to shake his hand, a flood of feelings swarmed over me. His statement couldn't have been any truer. It really was it. Lieutenant Colonel Quinn shook my hand firmly while, I am sure, my face was showing doubt. After the handshake, he signed my DD-214, and dismissed me for the last time.

I heard the phone ring as I left Lieutenant Colonel Quinn's office. I only remember that because of what he said. It struck me as odd. "He said no. Proceed as directed, and hurry it up."

With all that was happening, I did not follow that line of thought. Captain Kersey escorted me down the hallway towards the battalion HQ front doors as we caught up for a bit. This was starting to annoy me. I knew he was doing this to change my mind. Hell, I've known the guy for damn near eight years.

"Is White giving you a ride back to your truck?"

"Yes, but I haven't seen him anywhere."

"Are you sure I can't change your mind? Seriously, Bryan, are you really sure about this? Be absolutely sure about this."

"I am, Chris."

"My name's not Chris."

"What is it?"

"People will soon be calling me major, but your ugly ass can call me God."

"Oh Jesus Christ," I said.

We chuckled, as I gave him a firm handshake and

then a hug. He knew deep down I thought of him as an older brother, like Darrel from *The Outsiders*. The Marine Corps needs officers like him. Major-select Kersey took it upon himself to open the door for me. As I walked through, I heard him yell over my shoulder, "Atten-hut!"

The sound of boot heels simultaneously coming together echoed off the building walls. First, Second, and Third Platoons had formed two columns along the walkway out to the parking lot. It was touching and unexpected. I just stood there in the doorway, absolutely astonished. The shock of it had not hit me yet as I looked at Major-select Kersey.

Kersey grinned as he patted my back. "I'll walk you out."

As I passed each Marine, they softly said, "Thank you, gunny."

Major-select Kersey wanted their faces, the faces and voices of those I had saved, echoing in my head to remind me that one lost life saved many. He wanted that to resonate with me in case I started to feel a lack of self-worth. That was hard, really hard. I have never been thanked for anything, nor did I ever feel I was worthy.

As we walked, my head started filling with thoughts of changing my mind. Thick and thin, we had always been a tight group, and I was really going to miss these guys. This was my other family; they always will be.

At that point, I was wondering where White was, so I could get out of there before I really did change my mind. He wasn't anywhere I could see, but nevertheless, I continued on what seemed to be the longest walk ever. When we reached the end of the long walkway, I found out the reason the parking lot had been empty earlier.

"Battalion, atten-hut!"

And with that command, I watched in awe as the

entire First Reconnaissance Battalion came to the position of attention. It knocked the wind out of me. How do you react to something of this magnitude?

Normally, I could explain my thoughts, but not this time. I was so humbled by the gesture that words escaped me. This was such an emotional event that I even began to let myself cry a little. I tried very hard to hold it back, but my head slumped forward and my eyes really started tearing up. So there I stood, shedding some tears. Today was the day I learned that I truly had been given a gift.

That was the moment Lieutenant Colonel Quinn approached me. Unbeknownst to me, he had been in contact with his executive officer on whether or not to proceed with the farewell. This was, of course, contingent on my reversal of discharge, which I obviously did not do.

"It seemed prudent that we give one of the only seven Recon Marines to ever win the CMH a proper send-off," Lieutenant Colonel Quinn said to me as he held out an object. "On behalf of the battalion, we got you this as a parting gift."

When I looked up, Lieutenant Colonel Quinn handed me a plaque that the entire battalion had chipped in to get me. It had the unit insignia and a plate on it with a simple inscription:

ALWAYS STAY SWIFT, SILENT, AND DEADLY

SEMPER FI, MARINE

GUNNERY SERGEANT BRYAN "BEEZNUTS" BECZE

1995–2003

It was the moment that made me realize I was person-ally being thanked for every life I saved. Never in my life had I felt I made a difference. Here, in this moment, I was told otherwise. Lieutenant Colonel Quinn then shook my hand, came to attention, and saluted me.

Teary-eyed, I saluted back, and that truly was that.

It's a bothersome thing that most people think we Marines are just callous killers and have no heart. Let me clear up that misconception. It's our heart that makes us wear this uniform that stands for something bigger than us. It's our heart that allows us to know-ingly risk our lives in horrible places, for people we've never met and even for those that hate us. It's our heart that pushes us to go on when a brother of the sword dies, and the people back home couldn't care less. It's our heart that breaks when we see firsthand the evil that is wrought by humans all over the world. It's our heart that stops us from sharing those horrible experi-ences with our friends and families so we can shelter them from it. Most of all, it's our heart that shatters when we fail to help those who can't protect them-selves. Believe me, we are all heart. You only see the brick façade of we, the crazy tough.

There really isn't more I can say about that day other than White took me back to my brand-new 2003 Dodge Ram. I was going back to New Brunswick that evening.

Somehow, I was still troubled.

chapter fifteen

CLOSURE

The trip across America is an amazing adventure, which I highly recommend you make at least once in your life. The things you see remind you just how vast the country is and how small your bubble can be. The rock formations of Utah, Nevada, and Arizona. The Rocky Mountain views in Wyoming and Colorado. The flat land that never ends in Kansas, and so on. It is the idiosyncrasies of this nation that make it great.

Unfortunately for me, when I got to Plainsboro, New Jersey, particularly on Route 1 heading north, I was welcomed back by a Plainsboro cop who was kind enough to give me a speeding ticket within twenty minutes of crossing the border. The guy had a child-molester moustache and did not like me one bit. He even searched my vehicle. For what, I was unclear, as he refused to explain. What an asshole.

I had made the trip back to New Brunswick, and I had every intention of staying there and confessing my love to Maureen, like in some sort of a cheesy movie. However, I stopped at Fuddruckers on Route 1 North, because I had an overwhelming craving for one of their hamburgers. While I was waiting for my order, I looked north, towards the new Sony Cineplex that now occupied the plot of land where my beloved Route 1 Flea Market once sat, and I had an epiphany of sorts.

I was outdated.

This area had become so unfamiliar to me. I felt out of place and could not get my bearings. Even the Kendall Park Roller Rink was gone. A certain amount of change ought to be expected in the normal course of life, but it seemed everyplace where I once had an experience was now obliterated. All of a sudden, I felt like an outdated sense of fashion. Then it really hit me: why was I here?

I was disoriented by the time the person behind the counter brought me my order. As she handed it to me, I was in such in fog that she asked me if I was okay. Anxiety overpowered me as I got back in my truck. My meal sat on the passenger seat in its bag, as I stared off into space, with my hands on the steering wheel, squeezing it every few seconds. For reasons I cannot fathom, I began to drive north.

I had no idea where I was heading, I just knew I needed to go north. Somewhere between then and now, on I-95, it dawned on me to go to Big Moose Lake in the Adirondacks. I came to that decision once I had passed the Tappan Zee Bridge. Rick used to talk about that place, as his family had vacationed there every summer when he was a little kid. I had never gone once; by the time I came to live with them, they had stopped going. Call it intuition, but something was pulling me there; I had to go.

I veered off I-95N onto I-87N. It was on the on-ramp that I saw something that snapped me out of my head coma. On the side of the highway was a dog, trotting along with a limp. At first, I thought it was a shame. Then I realized there was a long fence along the highway and the only way that dog had gotten there was because somebody discarded it.

Initially, I had thought to keep on driving, but a gut-wrenching feeling stopped me. I pulled off onto the shoulder and got out of the truck as cars whizzed by. As I approached the dog, it acknowledged me by stopping, but as I whistled, moved towards me warily. From this distance, I could see it was malnourished and hadn't eaten anything in some time. Lucky for it, I hadn't yet eaten my Fuddruckers burger.

As it came closer, I could see it was a female and bred not long ago. She was uneasy, at first, so I had to kneel down and try to lure her over with the food. Eventually, she gave in, because the hunger was so great. So she limped over, and I was amazed. This creature had never seen me before, and had endured some serious shit at the hands of another human, but still was able to trust me enough to give her some food.

The closer she came, the more I knew she was a pit bull. What I had known, at least from the media, was that this was a vicious beast. Yet here was the gentlest creature, damaged, just like me. It was like it was meant to be, but she needed a vet, and fast.

I persuaded her to let me get her into my truck and head north. She devoured the meal in less than five minutes, including the fries. (No, there were no onions on the burger.)

There was a veterinarian hospital up the road about five miles, which the 411 operator was kind enough to look up for me. The dog sat in the passenger seat, gazing out through the windshield, as if she had always been my copilot, with the injured leg held up. As I looked at her, she looked at me, and her tail started slapping the seat. It almost looked like she was smiling.

Just to give you an idea about this beastly dog: she was all white with the exception of some black patches on her head. She had to have been about sixty pounds or so, but would probably be about eighty-something if she was healthy. We would find out soon enough.

As I pulled into the veterinarian hospital parking lot, I got out and walked around to the passenger side. I expected it would be a struggle to get her out of the truck, but she sat there looking at me. She then began to lick my face. It was at that point I knew I'd have to carry her.

When I came into the hospital, the vet assistant took out the paperwork and asked for her name. Realizing she had none that I knew of, I thought of something that meant perseverance of sorts. A vernacular genius I am not, but I remembered Major-select Kersey's favorite word, which I thought fitting: "Moxie." Then the vet assistant took her in the back while I waited.

After about an hour, a bunch of tests, and a shit-ton of X-rays, the vet called me into the back. Moxie lay there, panting, as the vet gave me her diagnosis. She had a fractured leg, quite a few infections, and heartworm. She was determined to be about a year old. I inquired of the vet what she personally would do in this situation. The vet told me she would do the "humane thing." In layman's terms, that meant she would put her down, and most people would have, after she gave me the estimate. The vet stressed that it would be the right thing to do. Who am I to argue with a veterinarian?

So, I made the decision.

SOUNDTRACK: Primitive Radio Gods, "Standing Outside a Broken Phone Booth"

I left the vet's office a changed man. As I plugged in my cassette adaptor for my CD player, I felt relieved in knowing I did the right thing, the only thing. As I hit a bump in the road, Moxie grunted to let me know that she disapproved of my driving.

People have often told me one way or another that I like to ice-skate uphill, and this was one of those occasions. Even with the painkillers and anesthesia running through her system, she was alert and panting a little. Just so you know, the bill came to $1,378.63 and it was a lot of money in 2003 for a stray dog, as I was told but I vehemently disagree. She was worth every cent. A dog's life is worth more than $1,400, and her smile made it worth it even more.

The veterinarian and her staff were so taken by my willingness to make sure Moxie lived that they put me in touch with someone local they knew who had a cabin for rent. I had saved up a decent amount of money, and the Marine Corps had given me a partial retirement pension on top of my CMH pension, so money was not an issue. Even though it was late evening, the cabin owner took my call and rented me the place immediately. Apparently, he was an old WWII vet himself, and knew my name from reading the papers. He left the key under the mat for me.

Moxie and I got to the cabin, and I was not disappointed at all. It was a small but quaint place; just like a studio apartment in the woods. Logs in the walls were stacked on top of each other, like the Abe Lincoln residence. America. The bed was against the wall, and there was a nice fireplace with a couch in front of it. An antique smell wafted through the place, and it was simple, but I found it very relaxing. Before I could even soak in the details, Moxie had hobbled in and somehow managed to get herself onto the bed and pass out. Her snoring was atrocious. Outstanding.

This place was perfect for decompressing. We must have stayed at that cabin for at least a good forty-five days. Every morning, Moxie and I would sit on the porch for a few hours. Without saying or doing anything, we would just sit and listen to the best soundtrack in the world: nature. No television, no radio, no cell phone, and no fucking Internet. Just nature. It was amazing.

In the afternoons, we hiked, with an occasional boat ride. Moxie was very calm on the water, but as of late, I developed a fear of open water. Don't ask, I have no idea why, but I suspect it probably has to do with my parachuting incident. They say that if you have a fear of heights, a fear of open water follows, and vice versa.

Every evening, I would read by the fireplace, and Moxie would sleep on me, no matter how uncomfortable it made me. I loved it though. She put me at ease. You could even say that she helped me more than I helped her. That was how it went for a while, and I needed this release from everything and everyone. Moxie made me feel human again.

However, I knew that I would eventually have to go home.

Meanwhile, back in New Brunswick, New Jersey . . .

Maureen sat on her parents' porch, looking out into the street, sipping coffee. She was stoic, but began to tear up. As much as she tried to fight it, she could not hold it back any longer. The pain of our situation finally broke her to some extent. Momma Calderra put her hand on Maureen's leg to comfort her as tears ran down her face.

"I don't get it. I have waited, and waited, and waited. Nothing, not a word? What did I do wrong?" Maureen asked.

Momma Calderra's heart broke as she watched her daughter agonize. She knew that Maureen could never shake off her love for me. The pain was inevitable, and Momma Calderra knew she needed to help Maureen stop loving me, not because I was an asshole, but because I was damaged. I understand now, particularly after Rick's funeral, that it was about protection.

"You did nothing. I've told you your whole life, he is broken. He is damaged. I have tried so hard to keep you from him, no matter how much you wanted him. Give it more time, baby. He will come around. Your father did after Vietnam," Momma Calderra said.

Maureen had been reeling from pain the entire time since she saw me last. This was it; the final straw. The moment had come for her to finally give up and move on to other things. She was just about to disagree with her mother, when she stopped.

SOUNDTRACK: The Flys, "Got You (Where I Want You)"

Her gaze was centered upon the street as she let the mug drop out of her hand. As it broke on the porch, she slowly stood up in disbelief. The coffee splashed everywhere. Momma Calderra jumped in her seat until she saw what Maureen was looking at. As Maureen started to walk down to the sidewalk, Momma Calderra cupped her hands over her face.

There I stood, on the sidewalk, with Moxie sitting on a leash doing her usual smiling bit while panting. Maureen slowly walked towards us as I just stood there like an idiot. I didn't rehearse this, nor did I think about it; I just did it.

With pain in her voice, she asked, "Where have you been?"

I started to regret this whole thing. Then I saw the look in Maureen's eyes. Call me less than manly, but that wilted me. She even managed to smile, which could melt a snowman in a blizzard. I looked at her and began to tear up a little bit.

"I . . . I just needed some time. I can't explain it. I just needed some time," I repeated.

Maureen looked at me angrily, as if she wanted to punch me, but then lightened up. For all the hell I had already put her through, she was ready to forgive me. That is madness, but according to *The Princess Bride*, that is true love. She looked at me and then at Moxie, then back at me, somewhat confused.

"Who's your friend?" she asked.

I looked at her, smiled, and responded, "This here is Moxie."

"Oh?" she said.

Moxie started wagging her tail. "She likes you," I added.

She started to cry a little, as she looked at me and said, "Just you, Bryan, just you."

She wanted to say something with feeling and value, but felt exhausted at this point. So she made it casual. "When do you go back to Cali—?"

I cut her off. "I'm not going back."

"Where did they stick you this time?"

"I got out."

Her face immediately went from sad to stunned. "What? But you love—"

I cut her off again, trying not to be emotional. "I

couldn't do it anymore, okay? I . . . I couldn't bury another friend, go on another pump overseas, or . . . or . . . or be away from you anymore."

I was just about to continue when I noticed Detective Lombardi across the street in his unmarked car. By the time I had locked eyes with him, he had started to swing the car around and now pulled up along the curb. This guy had been camped out across the street the whole time, in the hope that I would show up.

It was at this point that I knew I was fucked again.

He got out of the car, closed the door, leaned up against it, and began to gnaw on an apple. The sound of his chewing, open-mouthed, was obnoxious.

Detective Lombardi stood there for a minute, before finally asking, "Congressional Medal of Honor, eh?"

"Yes, detective," I answered.

"Now, that's some serious hero shit right there. Seems you saved the lives of over eighty-some Marines, right?" he continued through a mouth full of apple.

"Ninety, actually. Yes."

"You just keep on saving people, huh, here and abroad?"

I looked confused, but he continued.

"Damnedest thing about your buddy Vinnie. Forensics said, and witnesses concur, he slipped and hit his head on the corner of that table, causing severe trauma on the back of his head, which, in turn, caused an aneurysm, killing him instantly."

I knew better, and, without catching on, began to correct the detective. "But, detective, that table was flimsy aluminum and the plastic—"

He cut me off. "Those tables are known for their sturdiness. It's amazing the amount of deaths they have caused over the years. It's really quite tragic." He shot me a look to make sure I understood his point. "I'd re-member that if I were you. Know what I mean? Any-way, my report was pretty thorough."

I nodded, as he let a small smirk escape and contin-ued, "Just wanted to shake the hand of a living CMH recipient. I think it's going to be nice and quiet around here for a while. A man could get used to that, espe-cially when he is three years from retirement. *Semper fi,* Marine."

Brotherhood. Before I could thank the detective, he sped off. What a load off my shoulders. Perhaps this was a sign of new beginnings.

SOUNDTRACK: Hum, "Stars"

Maureen hastily walked over to me and hugged me tightly, almost suffocating me. She was relieved. So was I, but I have never been one to express any positivity. With her head on my shoulder, she cried out all the frustration of years past. When she was done, she looked me in the eye, sniffling, and ran her fingers through my hair, which I had let grow out. "Always a day late and a dollar short. You can finally say you love me, you know?"

I was emotionally exhausted, but felt an enormous joy.

I simply replied, "Always and forever."

Ten years have passed since that day, and, as with all things in life, change has happened. Moxie is still with us, thankfully. Eventually, I went to college at Rutgers and got my bachelor's, then my MBA. Maureen and I got married and I did the one thing I said I'd never do: had kids.

It was as if the universe had wanted some sort of payback for my previous misadventures with women, and decided to award me two of the most energetic and precocious little girls. Samantha, the eldest at an adult age of five, knew everything about everything already, and Stacey is three going on seven. I made an oath that their future boyfriends know that anything they do to my girls I will do to them. That ought to keep them honest.

The only reason I had stayed in New Jersey was for the sake of the Calderra family. Poppa Calderra died three years ago of a heart attack and Momma Calderra passed less than a year ago from pancreatic cancer. She was by far one of the toughest women I have ever known. Case in point, she was given three months and lasted a year and seven months; the warrior queen.

I have visited Rick's grave every year since he was buried, on his birthday and on Thanksgiving, because it was our favorite holiday, but today was different. Today was the day I was asking his permission to leave indefinitely. It may sound strange to you, but I had to ask permission. You see, we Marines don't die, our spirits watch over each other from the halls of Valhalla. Sometimes our guardian whispers in the ears of our brethren to guide us on the right path. That is why I am here today.

So here I was, for the first time with the whole family: Maureen, Sammy, and Stacey. I wanted the girls to finally meet their uncle. However, they saw nothing but a headstone.

As I stood alone now before Rick's gravestone, I looked down at it in silence. About ten minutes passed, and I stood there quietly, not uttering a word. I used to be able to speak to him without an issue, but not in this moment. Of all the times I have come here, this is the one that affected me the most. Out of respect, loyalty, and love, I had to ask him if I could leave. So, I begun.

"Hey, buddy. I brought the family this time so you could finally meet them. Don't know why I haven't brought them before." I paused. "On another note, I hope you are bothering the shit out of Mom and Dad." I snickered.

It took me a second to catch my breath so I could continue. "I came here because I need to ask you something important. I got a job offer in Texas, and it's a good opportunity. Yeah, Texas . . ."

I looked up and around at the skyline of New Brunswick.

"I want a better life for my kids, better than ours. I mean, we're leaving, but I wanted to ask you anyway. It . . .it . . . it just doesn't feel right otherwise."

I looked back down at his headstone. "I know

you're watching over us now, and I need your blessing. Just give me something, anything to let me know it's okay. It's time we go, bro. It's time we go. I need to go."

I waited for what felt like an eternity. I could feel Maureen and the kids growing a little impatient, but they stayed cool. Silence surrounded me otherwise.

I looked around once again to see if there was something, anything, that would give me an indication that somehow Rick was able to reach through the spirit world and let me know his approval. It was crazy to think, especially as an agnostic for most of my life. Yet here I was, believing—no, hoping—that there was a hint of support in my decision.

I started to fall back to reality. I nodded in disappointment and shook my right hand as if I had loose change in it. Exhaling deeply, I turned to walk back towards Maureen. I must have made it five or six steps when I heard it.

The flapping of wings got faster as the bird adjusted its landing onto the top of Rick's gravestone. I turned around quickly, mostly because I was startled, but beheld the majestic winged soul-carrier as it stood atop the gravestone. A raven. It was a fucking raven.

I stood in amazement as the raven quickly hopped from side to side across the top of the gravestone. Its head kept swinging back and forth quickly, to look at me through both eyes. It let out a loud caw and then took off.

I watched the raven fly off towards the unkindness of other ravens, and I nodded softly. A sort of warmth came over me as the stress I felt was now ebbing away.

"Thanks, bro," I said with a small grin on my face.

I turned back, and Samantha was now standing in front of me.

"What were you doing, Daddy?"

"Saying goodbye to your guardian angel," I responded with a slight smile.

We held hands as we walked up to Maureen and Stacey. I hugged them both, and we began our walk out of the cemetery. I glanced around one more time, just to get a final look. For the first time in my life, I was no longer wondering, what if? Rather, I began to wonder, what now?

I have always been asked, "Have you ever regretted joining the Marine Corps?"

My answer is always the same, "Not—one—fucking—bit."

SOUNDTRACK: Kanye West, "Jesus Walks"

SEMPER FIDELIS

Oh, Lord, please keep my Marine tonight,
Close by Your guiding hand of might,
Give him the strength to carry on
When all is dark and hope is gone.
Help him to trust and have no fear
For You are watching, ever near.
Let him know that he's not alone;
Your light will always lead him home.
He's rough and tough—no emotions show—
But, God, he's just a man, you know.
He claims the title and wears it proud;
Says he's the best and says it loud.
And though someday he'll guard Your heights,
Lord, please bring him safely home tonight.

~ Author unknown ~

Bryan W. Becze was born in New Brunswick, New Jersey, and graduated from North Brunswick Township High School. He lived in Princeton and North Brunswick throughout his young life. Bryan spent eight years in the United States Marine Corps and participated in Operations Stabilise (AU), Enduring Freedom, and Iraqi Freedom. He is a world-travelled shellback (U.S. Navy).

Upon completing his time in the USMC, Bryan attended DeVry University in North Brunswick, New Jersey, earning a Bachelor of Science in Business Administration with a focus on project management. He has a Master of Political Management (MPM) degree from George Washington University and a Master of Business Administration (MBA) from Rutgers School of Business–Camden, magna cum laude.

Currently, Bryan is enrolled in the Master of Science in Enterprise Risk Management program at Columbia University.

Bryan is an avid animal lover and supports multiple organizations that benefit animals. A keen eco-conservationist, he lives in New Jersey with his longtime girlfriend, Kristin, and their two pit bulls, Athena and Dakota. He is an avid fan of the Boston Red Sox, New Jersey Devils, and collegiate football.

Made in the USA
Monee, IL
02 July 2020

35474156R10125